"I'd Love To Taste Your Chocolate," Chase Said, Keeping His Gaze Directed On Her.

Jessica swallowed as a sharp physical sensation sliced through her. She wondered if they were still discussing the same thing. "There's some left on the stove," she said.

Chase followed her to the kitchen and watched as she stuck her hand in the pot, then tasted the chocolate from her finger.

At the sight of her licking her finger clean Chase felt his control begin to slip. "May I have a taste?" he asked, shrugging out of his leather jacket and walking toward her.

"Sure. Is a spoonful okay or do you want—"

"I want you," Chase said, as he came to stand in front of her. She smelled good, but he knew she'd taste even better....

Dear Reader,

It's November and perhaps the weather is turning a bit cooler where you are…so why not heat things up with six wonderful Silhouette Desire novels? *New York Times* bestselling author Diana Palmer is back this month with a LONG, TALL TEXANS story not to be missed. You've loved Blake Kemp and his ever-faithful assistant, Violet, in other books…. Now you finally get their love story, in *Boss Man*.

Heat continues to generate in DYNASTIES: THE ASHTONS with Laura Wright's contribution, *Savor the Seduction*. Grant and Anna shared a night of passion some months ago…now he's wondering if they have a shot at a repeat performance. And the temperature continues to rise as Sara Orwig delivers her share of surprises, in *Highly Compromised Position,* the latest installment in the TEXAS CATTLEMAN'S CLUB: THE SECRET DIARY series. (Hint, someone in Royal, Texas, is pregnant!)

Brenda Jackson gets things simmering in *The Chase Is On,* another fabulous Westmoreland story with a strong emphasis on food…tasty! And Bronwyn Jameson is back with the conclusion of her PRINCES OF THE OUTBACK series. Who wouldn't want to share body heat with *The Ruthless Groom?* Last but not least, get all hot and bothered in the boardroom with Margaret Allison's business-becomes-pleasure holiday story, *Mistletoe Maneuvers.*

Here's hoping you find plenty of ways to keep yourself warm. Enjoy all we have to offer at Silhouette Desire.

Best,

Melissa Jeglinski

Melissa Jeglinski
Senior Editor
Silhouette Books

Please address questions and book requests to:
Silhouette Reader Service
U.S.: 3010 Walden Ave., P.O. Box 1325, Buffalo, NY 14269
Canadian: P.O. Box 609, Fort Erie, Ont. L2A 5X3

BRENDA JACKSON

THE CHASE IS ON

Silhouette® Desire

Published by Silhouette Books

America's Publisher of Contemporary Romance

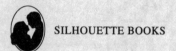 **SILHOUETTE BOOKS**

ISBN 0-373-76690-4

THE CHASE IS ON

Copyright © 2005 by Brenda Streater Jackson

BRENDA JACKSON

is a die "heart" romantic who married her childhood sweetheart and still proudly wears the "going steady" ring he gave her when she was fifteen. Because she's always believed in the power of love, Brenda's stories always have happy endings. In her real-life love story, Brenda and her husband of thirty-three years live in Jacksonville, Florida, and have two sons.

A *USA TODAY* bestselling author, Brenda divides her time between family, writing and working in management at a major insurance company. You may write Brenda at P.O. Box 28267, Jacksonville, Florida, 32226, by e-mail at WriterBJackson@aol.com or visit her Web site at www.brendajackson.net.

Acknowledgments

To Gerald Jackson, Sr., my husband and hero.

To Joyce Perry, who told me everything I needed
to know about making chocolate…even some
things I really didn't need to know.
Thanks, JP!

An unreliable messenger can cause a lot of trouble
Reliable communication permits progress.
—*Proverbs* 13:17

Prologue

Eighteen years ago

"**N**ever trust a Graham."

Sixteen-year old Chase Westmoreland slid onto the stool at the counter in his grandfather's restaurant. The old man turned and spoke while placing a huge glass of milk and a plate filled with cookies in front of him.

"Why? What's wrong, Gramps?" Chase asked as he immediately attacked the stack of cookies.

"What's wrong? I'll tell you what's wrong. Carlton Graham stole some of our secret recipes and passed them on to Donald Schuster."

Chase stopped eating as his eyes grew large. He knew how his grandfather felt about the Westmoreland family recipes. They had been in the family for generations. "But Mr. Graham is your friend."

Scott Westmoreland frowned at his grandson. "Not anymore he isn't. Our friendship ended along with our partnership two weeks ago. I never thought I'd live to see the day he would betray me this way."

Chase downed a huge gulp of milk and then asked, "Are you sure he did it?"

Scott Westmoreland nodded, his features tired and full of pain and disappointment. "Yes, I'm sure. I'd heard that Schuster had added a couple of new dishes to his menu that taste just like mine, so I went to investigate for myself."

Chase nodded. "And?"

"They're mine all right. Schuster won't say where he got the recipes, but I knew they are mine."

Chase sadly shook his head. He'd always liked Mr. Graham and his chocolate chip cookies were the best. His grandfather's were all right, but Mr. Graham's had a special ingredient that made them mouth-wateringly delicious. "Did you ask Mr. Graham about it?"

"Of course I did and he denies everything, but I know he's lying. He's the only person who knows exactly what ingredients I use. He must feel guilty. That's probably the reason he's not wasting any time moving his family out of town."

Chase's eyes widened. "The Grahams are moving away?"

"Yes and good riddance. It wouldn't bother me any if I never saw another Graham again. Like I said, they can't be trusted. Always remember that."

One

The present

He needed an attitude adjustment.

That thought flashed through Chase Westmoreland's mind as he turned the corner to pull into his restaurant's parking lot. Six months of abstinence, he concluded, had to be the reason he'd been in such a bad mood lately.

It had nothing to do with the fact that in the last three years, all of his four brothers and his baby sister had gotten married. Even his cousin Jared, the die-hard bachelor and divorce lawyer, had recently fallen victim. Chase was sick and tired of varied family members looking at him with a knowing smile on their lips. If they were waiting for him to be next, then they had a long wait ahead of them.

And it didn't help matters that his brothers were cocky enough to say he would change his mind when the right woman came along. His comeback to them had been quick and confident. The "right woman" didn't exist.

"What the hell!" He brought his car to a sudden stop in the middle of the parking lot outside his restaurant, which was buzzing with activity. He had forgotten that someone had purchased the building a few doors from Chase's Place. From the way things looked, they were moving in.

He had received notice a few weeks ago that he would have a new neighbor.

He wasn't surprised. Atlanta was a city of international renown that had managed to hold on to its southern charm. And the downtown section where his restaurant was located with its charming neighborhoods, tree-shaded streets and friendly communities, made it a prime area for doing business. If he remembered correctly, someone would be opening a confectionery.

When he'd first heard about it, the news had brought out his cravings for chocolate, but now seeing the mass of confusion surrounding him all thoughts of sweets suddenly turned sour.

Moving trucks were everywhere and taking up parking spaces his customers would need. It was barely six in the morning and he had a huge breakfast crowd. The last thing he needed was someone messing with the availability of parking. It was a good thing he had a reserved spot in front of his restaurant, or there wouldn't be any space left even for him.

He sat in his car, forcing himself to breath calmly as a truck blocked him in. This was Monday, not a good day for his patience to be tested. He was just about to hit his horn when a woman walking out of the building caught his attention. For a moment he forgot his anger. Hell, he even forgot to breathe.

As she talked to the driver of the truck blocking his path, he looked her up and down. She was a prime specimen of a woman. She was dressed in a short baker's smock, and he hoped she had on a pair of shorts since a good gust of wind would show him and anyone else what may or may not be underneath. A smile drifted over his lips. Even with the smock he could tell she had one helluva figure. And when his gaze lit on her face...

His skin suddenly felt overheated as he looked into a medium brown face too beautiful for words. She had a pair of honey-brown eyes and full, moist lips covered in what looked like juicy red strawberry lip gloss. He wanted to get out of his car, walk over to her and kiss the coloring right off her lips. Then there was her hair, a mass of dark-brown curls that tumbled over her shoulders. For the first time in quite a while Chase found himself physically affected by a beautiful woman.

That thought made him take a deep breath and he forced himself to pull back. He was a thirty-four-year-old hot-blooded male and there was nothing wrong with responding to visual stimuli. But he couldn't let a great pair of legs and a gorgeous face scatter his wits. All he had to do was remember his last year at Duke University and Iris Nelson. Thinking of Iris made warning bells go off...the sound of reason.

Sighing deeply, he let his gaze drift over her once more before backing up his car and moving around the truck. He sighed, glad he was breathing again. As soon as he got inside his restaurant he would drink a strong cup of black coffee.

Chase only wished he hadn't noticed the absence of a wedding ring on the woman's finger, making him happier than it ought to.

Jessica Claiborne smiled as she looked around her shop. After moving in she was already set for the shop's grand opening tomorrow morning. She had spent the day doing last-minute checks on inventory and confirming arrangement for deliveries. She had hired two high-school students to pass out flyers about the shop around the community. Since she intended for all of her products to be baked fresh daily, she had made a call to the children's hospital and offered to donate any treats she didn't sell tomorrow. Also, she had signed contracts with a couple of the hotels around town to supply their restaurants and coffeeshops with baked goods.

She glanced out the window. It was a beautiful day in early October. The movers had gotten everything set up on Monday and the artist she'd hired had come that morning to paint her shop's name on the display window. Delicious Cravings was the name she had decided on, and she would be forever thankful to her grandmother for making her dream come true.

Sadness settled in Jessica's heart whenever she thought about the grandmother she had simply adored and the inheritance she'd been left when her grandmother had died last year on Jessica's twenty-fifth birthday. The money had made it possible to walk away from her stressful job as a corporate attorney in Sacramento and pursue her dream of owning and operating her own confectionery.

She sniffed the air, enjoying the smell of chocolate cooking. Already today she had made a batch of assorted pastries including éclairs and tarts. But what she had enjoyed more than anything was whipping up chocolate nut clusters and an assortment of cookies for her neighbors as an apology for inconveniencing them during her move.

Mrs. Morrison who owned the seamstress shop next door had accepted her apology but declined her treats since she was allergic to chocolate but had said she would love to try her shortcake. The Criswell brothers, who owned the karate school, had accepted her gift and apology graciously, welcomed her to the strip and said they looked forward to patronizing her shop. The only person left was the owner of Chase's Place. Jessica hoped the restaurateur was just as understanding as Mrs. Morrison and the Criswell brothers had been and that he had a sweet tooth.

Grabbing the box she had filled with sweet treats, she walked out the door and locked it behind her. She had hired a part-time helper, an elderly woman who would come in during the busy lunchtime hours.

It was early afternoon but she could tell the restaurant was packed and hoped the business would eventually trickle over to her once people realized she was open. Before she got within ten feet of the restaurant she could smell the mouth-watering food and realized she hadn't eaten anything since breakfast.

She walked into Chase's Place, immediately liking what she saw. It was a very upscale restaurant that somehow maintained a homey atmosphere. Lanterns adorned each table and the tablecloths matched curtains that hung in the windows. There was a huge counter with bar stools and soft jazzy music coming from a speaker located somewhere in the back.

"Welcome to Chase's Place, where you're guaranteed to get the finest in soul food. Are you dining in or carrying out?"

Jessica smiled at the young woman who greeted her. "I'm the owner of the new confectionery a few doors down and wanted to bring the owner a gift for any inconvenience he might have encountered while I was moving in."

The woman nodded. "That would be Chase and he's in his office. If you follow me I'll show you the way."

"Thanks."

Jessica followed the woman down a hall that led to the back of the restaurant. Everything looked tidy, even the storage room they passed. The hostess knocked when they reached the office door. "Who is it?" a deep, husky voice called out.

"It's Donna. Someone is here to see you."

"Hell, I'm surprised anyone can get through with all that chaos that's been going on in the parking lot. I have a good mind to go over there and give my inconsiderate new neighbor a piece of my mind for all the problems she's caused me the last couple of days. I couldn't get my own deliveries through for—"

Chase stopped talking when his door swung open

and the woman he had checked out Monday morning walked into his office past a speechless Donna. "I guess I've saved you a trip. I would think, considering the circumstances, you would have been just as understanding as my other neighbors and…"

Whatever the woman was saying Chase had stopped listening mere seconds after she walked into his office. Heat flared through all parts of his body and his full concentration centered on the shorts and tank top she was wearing.

Up close her legs were more of a turn-on than they had been on Monday morning. He blinked. The closer she got, the better she looked, especially those moist strawberry lips. She was angry…sexy as hell.

In addition to the honey-brown eyes and curly dark hair that tumbled around her face, she possessed perfect cheekbones and a cute perky nose. He couldn't help noticing that the mouth that was moving was beautifully shaped and ready to be kissed.

"And I hope you choke on these!"

He was jolted from his lust-filled thoughts when a box was suddenly shoved against his chest. It took only a split second for him to realize his visitor was leaving. When the door slammed shut, he looked at Donna, ignored the silly smirk on her face and asked, "What the hell did she say?"

He watched Donna's try to hide a laugh. "I think, boss, that you've been thoroughly told off. I can't believe you weren't listening."

No, he hadn't been listening. He looked down at the box.

"That was supposed to be a peace offering," Donna explained. "She came to apologize for the inconvenience over the past couple of days. I think that was downright neighborly of her. I guess she hoped you'd be more understanding of the chaos she caused while moving in."

Chase nodded, suddenly filled with regret that he hadn't been more understanding. But he'd been in a foul mood for the past week and had wrongly directed his anger at her. She was a woman after all, and a woman, or actually the lack of one, was the root of his problem.

Granted he wasn't the ladies' man his twin brother Storm had been, but usually he could pull out his little phone book and contact any number of women, who, like him, were more interested in getting down than getting married. But for some reason doing so didn't suit him. The last woman he dated had read more into the relationship and he'd had one hell of a time convincing her that bedding her didn't mean he'd be wedding her. He wasn't into serious relationships of any kind and had told her that in the beginning. Evidently somewhere along the way she'd forgotten.

He dragged a weary hand down his face. Some women saw the single Westmoreland men as challenges. His brother Storm's philosophy—before his wife Jayla had entered his life—had been that he enjoyed women too much to settle down with just one. Chase believed in learning from his mistakes, and his biggest one had been a woman by the name of Iris Nelson.

While in college at Duke, he had seemed headed for

a pro basketball career when an injury had ended his dreams. He'd found himself facing an endless future when Iris, the girl he had fallen in love with, decided that with no chance at the pros he was no longer a good prospect.

Over the years he'd become wary of opportunistic women who only entered relationships to find out what was in it for them, and when the going got tough, they got going. Making women secondary in his life was the best way to eliminate the chance of a repeat heartbreak.

"So what are you going to do?" Donna asked, interrupting his thoughts.

He didn't have a clue. One thing was certain, he owed his new neighbor an apology. "Tell Kevin to prepare a today's special to go and be generous with the servings."

Chuckling, Donna nodded. "You think you'll find her soft spot with food?"

He looked down at the box he held in his hand and inhaled the aroma of chocolate. "Wasn't that her game plan?"

Donna gave him a long look before slowly shaking her head and closing the door behind her as she left.

Chase placed the box on his desk. The top was marked Delicious Cravings. He thought of how she'd looked Monday morning when he had first seen her and just moments ago standing in the middle of his office. The name was definitely appropriate.

He opened the box and immediately fell in love—with the sweets. Yes, he definitely owed the woman an apology and before the evening ended he would make sure she got one.

* * *

That man had a bad attitude!

Jessica took a deep breath, refusing to get any more upset than she already was. How dare he say she was inconsiderate? She was one of the most considerate people she knew. It was one of the reasons she had walked away from her high-paying job as a corporate attorney.

She had gotten fed up with having to fight for things she didn't believe in, pushing policies that ruined people's lives, being forced to put corporate profits before the consumers' best interests.

And her consideration for her family's wishes was the only thing pushing her to seek out members of the Westmoreland family to right a wrong made against her family years ago. The nerve of them thinking her grandfather had been a dishonest man! He had been one of the most honest men she knew and if it was left up to her, she would give the Westmorelands a good piece of her mind and tell them just what she thought of their accusations. But before taking her final breath her grandmother had made her promise to come to Atlanta to clear the Graham name without starting World War III, and she intended to do that. After doing research on the area, she decided Atlanta would be a good place to live and not just visit. And so she had made the decision to relocate to the area.

She sighed as her thoughts drifted back to the owner of Chase's Place. He had reminded her of dark chocolate of the richest kind and she knew one of the reasons she had gone off on him the way she had was that she couldn't afford to get caught up in his sheer beauty. Even with his horrible attitude she had to admit that he was handsome as sin. Taller and well-built, his features took her breath away. He had reminded her that she was a woman, something she often tried to forget.

The last thing she needed was to get attracted to a man. She refused to get so carried away that she forgot how deceitful they were. She had learned her lesson even if her mother never had. Jeff Claiborne may have been the man who had fathered her, but he was also the man who had kept her mother dangling on a string for over fifteen years with promises of marriage. When Jessica had been born he had given her his name, but her mother's last name had remained Graham.

It had taken her grandfather's paid investigator to deliver the news that there was no way Jeff Claiborne could ever marry Janice Graham. He was already married to another woman and had a family living in Philadelphia. The news had been a terrible blow to her mother—one that she had never recovered from. She took her own life rather that live with the heartache and pain.

At the age of fifteen Jessica had watched as her mother's coffin was lowered into the ground and had vowed never to give her heart to any man. She wouldn't be fooled by a man as deceitful as her father had been, one man who could take undying love and abuse it in the worst possible way.

Her grandfather, angry and hurt over what Jeff Claiborne had done, had made sure the man didn't get away unscathed. He had paid a visit to Jeff Claiborne's wife and had presented her with documented proof of her husband's duplicity. Jennifer Claiborne, a good woman, hadn't wasted any time filing for a divorce and leaving her husband of eighteen years. And Jennifer had gone one step further by welcoming Jessica into her family, making sure she got to know her sister and brother, and making sure Jeff Claiborne contributed to her support. She knew Jennifer had been instrumental in helping to set up the college fund that had been available when she had graduated from high school.

Savannah and Rico were as close to her as any brother and sister could be. And Jennifer was like a second mother to her. She'd known she could always go visit her extended family in Philadelphia.

Jessica heard a knock at the door and frowned. Dusk was settling in but she could plainly see through her display window that her unexpected visitor was the man from the restaurant.

She had a good mind to ignore him. For the last couple of weeks since moving to Atlanta she had begun thinking she had finally found peace, but now he was convincing her otherwise.

She heard his knock again and decided that she wouldn't hide. Like everything else in life she would deal with her problems, and in this case, her problem was him. He had sought her out and she supposed she needed to make nice because she'd be seeing him a lot. This building was not only the place she would work but thanks to space above the shop, it was also her new home.

Deciding she had let him linger long enough, she made her way to the door and unlocked it. She took a deep breath before opening it. "What do you want?"

He had been standing with his back to her, looking up at the sky. The day had been beautiful but it seemed that tonight it would rain. He turned around and as soon as their gazes locked she felt the temperature go up about one hundred degrees.

He still reminded her of rich dark chocolate rum balls but now something else had been added to the mixture, she thought, as her gaze moved from the base-ball cap on his head to the features in his face. A slight indention in the bridge of his nose indicated it may have been broken at one time but she didn't even consider that a flaw. Nothing, and she meant nothing, distracted from this man's good looks.

Jeeze. That wasn't a good sign.

And to make matters worse, his smile was so potent that she was forced to grip the doorknob to support her suddenly wobbly knees. Forcing her eyes away from that smile, she met his gaze once more and it angered her that he had this kind of effect on her. "I repeat, what do you want?" she all but snapped.

His grin widened. He was either oblivious to her less-than-friendly mood or else he chose to ignore it. "I came to apologize and to deliver a peace offering," he said, widening that killer smile even more and holding up a bag that smelled of delicious food.

"I was out of line earlier," he said. "And I do under-stand how it is moving in. The only excuse I can give for my behavior is that this has been one hell of a week. But my problems are not your fault."

His apology surprised her, but it didn't captivate her

as he had evidently assumed it would. Long ago she had learned to be cautious of smooth-talking men.

"Will you accept my apology?"

She jutted her chin. "Why should I?"

"Because it will prove that you're a much nicer person than I am and someone with a forgiving spirit."

Jessica leaned against the doorjamb, thinking that she was definitely a much nicer person than he, but she wasn't all that sure about having a forgiving spirit. She inhaled deeply, deciding she didn't want to accept his apology. She didn't like the chemistry she felt flowing between them and she also decided she didn't like him. She knew it all sounded irrational, but at the moment she didn't care. "There are a lot of things I can overlook, but rudeness isn't one of them."

Chase lifted a brow and frowned. "So you aren't going to accept my apology?"

She glared at him. "At the moment, no."

His frown deepened as he peered down at her. "Why?"

"Because I don't feel like it. Now if you'll excuse me I need to—"

He held up a hand, cutting her off. "Because you don't feel like it?"

"That's what I said."

Chase felt frustration take over his body. He had dealt with many unreasonable people, but this woman gave new meaning to the word. Yes, he had been rude. But he had apologized, hadn't he?

"Look," he said slowly, while trying to overlook the irritation plastered on her face. "I know things got off to a bad start between us, and for that I apologize. And you're right. I was rude, but now you're the one who is being unreasonable."

Jessica sighed deeply. The dark-brown eyes focused on hers were intense, sharp, and to-die-for, but still…

"But still nothing, Jessica Lynn," she could hear her grandmother saying in the recesses of her mind. *"You can't judge every man by your father. You can't continue to put up this brick wall against any man who gets too close."*

Sighing again, she smoothed a hand down her face. Her grandmother was right but the need to protect herself had always been elemental. For some reason she had an inkling that the man standing before her was someone she should avoid at all costs.

"Please accept my peace offering as I did yours, okay?" Chase asked, interrupting her thoughts. "By the way, everything was delicious, especially the chocolate chip cookies. They're my favorite and I haven't tasted chocolate chip cookies that delicious in years. They were melt-in-your-mouth delicious." He slanted her a smile. "And I didn't choke on any of them."

"Too bad," she said dryly. Their gazes held for a moment, and she knew she was a puzzle he was trying to figure out. No doubt other women didn't cause him any trouble. He probably flashed his smile and got whatever he wanted. Just like her father.

She wrapped her arms around herself knowing he didn't intend to leave until she accepted his apology. "Okay, I accept your apology. Goodbye."

He grabbed the door before she could slam it shut in

his face. He held up the bag and smiled. "And the peace offering?"

She snorted a breath. "And the peace offering," she said reaching for the bag.

Chase chuckled. "Now we're getting somewhere." Instead of giving her the bag he held his hand out to her. "We haven't been properly introduced. I'm Chase Westmoreland. And you are?" he asked taking her hand.

Jessica knew if she had a lighter skin tone he would have seen all the blood drain from her face. "Westmoreland?"

He grinned. "Yes, does the name ring a bell? There's a bunch of us living in Atlanta."

Deciding she wasn't ready to tell him just how familiar it was, she shook her head. "No, I recently moved here from California."

He nodded and after a few moments he said smiling, "You never told me your name."

She blinked, recalling that she hadn't. "I'm Jessica Claiborne."

His smile widened. "Welcome to Atlanta, Jessica. Do you have family here?"

"No," she answered truthfully, "I have no family living here." Her head was still spinning at the realization that he was a Westmoreland.

There was a bit of silence between them when Chase remembered the bag he was holding. "Oops, I almost forgot. Here you go," he said handing the bag to Jessica. "It's today's special. I hope you enjoy it."

"Thanks."

He hesitated for a moment then said, "I guess I'd better get back. The dinner crowd is arriving. Will you be living upstairs?"

"Yes," she said, gripping the bag in both hands. She needed to get away from him to think.

"Well, every once in a while if it's a late night, I sleep over my place, too. If you ever need anything, just let me know."

Don't hold your breath, Jessica thought, closing the door on temptation.

Two

Jessica leaned back in the chair and licked her lips. That had to have been the most delicious meal she'd eaten in a very long time. The smothered pork chops had been tender, just the way she liked and the mashed potatoes had made her groan out loud. No wonder Chase's Place was packed. The dessert, a slice of carrot cake, had been melt-in-your-mouth delicious. And she knew baked goods. Her grandmother had been the best baker she'd ever met.

She'd always enjoyed baking because of all the times she had spent with her grandparents in the kitchen growing up. She had even considered going to culinary school instead of law school. But her grandfather had talked her out of it, saying there were enough cooks in the Graham family.

As she cleaned up, Jessica glanced around her apartment. It was just the right size for her, with a large living room, a bath, a small kitchen and a bedroom. She loved the hardwood floors and the huge window in the living room.

She smiled at the thought that she actually owned this place, the entire building. Downstairs in the shop, there was a huge cooking area and a small office in the back. It had been just what she'd been looking for. According to the real estate agent, all the buildings were newly renovated and business in the area was always good. She moved over to the window and glanced out again at all the people gathered at Chase's Place.

Her breath suddenly caught when she noticed Chase walk out of his restaurant with another man. It was plain to see the two were related since there were distinct similarities in their features. But Chase was the one holding her attention. The sun had gone down, but the faint light illuminated him. He looked good in his jeans and black pullover shirt, and even from where she was standing she could see his perfectly chiseled features.

She sighed deeply, and as if he had heard, he glanced toward her window and their eyes met. She felt it, the moment their eyes connected, a jolt in the lower part of her body, a current of electricity that spiked up her spine. Both feelings suddenly rejuvenated that part of her that had been dormant since her first year of college. The one and only time she'd ever had sex had been an awful experience she hadn't ever wanted to repeat.

But now, looking at Chase perpetuated more than mild curiosity; for a single moment she wondered if making love with him would be different. She blinked, and stepped away from the window. How could she have forgotten just who Chase was? He was a West-moreland, for heaven's sake! She refused to become a lust-crazed lunatic over someone from a family of liars who had accused her grandfather of being a thief. It didn't matter to her that Chase was the epitome of everything male. He was a Westmoreland and that meant he was definitely off-limits.

"Who is she?"

A smile caught the corner of Chase's mouth as his attention was drawn from the window where Jessica had been standing back to his brother Storm. "Need I remind you that you're married?" Chase replied.

Storm chuckled as he shook his head. "No. Jayla is the love of my life and all the woman I'd ever need, and the girls are the icing on the cake," he said of his three-month-old twin daughters. "But it seems to me that she has gotten your attention."

The smile faded from Chase's lips. Jessica Claiborne had definitely caught his attention and from the moment they met. "Her name is Jessica Claiborne. We didn't hit it off at first."

Storm's lips tilted in amused humor. "And now?"

Chase leaned against the building. "I think she still doesn't like me."

Storm lifted his brows. "First impressions can be changed if you work hard at it," he said as he watched his brother's gaze shift back to the window where the woman had been standing earlier. He glanced at his watch. "I have to go. I just wanted to make sure you knew about the christening on Sunday."

"Yes, Mom mentioned it. I think the restaurant is perfect for the after-christening dinner."

Storm smiled. "Are you sure? I wouldn't want you to go to any trouble."

"No trouble for my nieces. Consider it done. Tell Jayla that I'll call her sometime tomorrow to discuss the menu."

"Ok, I'll do that."

Chase watched his twin brother get into his car and pull away. He hesitated for a moment not ready to go back inside and glanced at the confectionery again, wondering whether Jessica had enjoyed the meal he'd had prepared for her. There was only one way to find out.

Shoving his hands into his pockets he walked past Mrs. Morrison's seamstress shop until he stood directly in front of Delicious Cravings. Ignoring the Closed sign on the door, he knocked a couple of times then rang the doorbell. Moments later a soft voice asked. "Who is it?"

"Chase."

She slowly opened the door and glared at him. "What do you want now?"

The bitterness that was still in her voice surprised him. He would have thought that if his apology hadn't done the trick, certainly a meal from Chase's Place had smoothed her over. Evidently not. He heaved a sigh.

She had folded her arms over her chest and he wished she hadn't done that. Although he was a leg man first, he was a breast man second and the position of her arms clearly empathized what a nice, firm, full pair she had. At that moment he actually envied her tank top.

He cleared his throat and said, "I saw you standing at the window."

Her gaze sharpened. "So?"

He smoothed a hand across his forehead. Maybe where she came from, people were unfriendly and unpleasant, but here in the South people were warm and gracious. "Is it too much to hope that you enjoyed dinner?" he asked.

She actually seemed surprised by his question. "Of course I enjoyed dinner. Why would you think that I hadn't?"

"Your attitude."

Jessica clamped down her jaw down from jutting out. Okay, so once again he hadn't seen her at her best, but there was a reason for it. He was a Westmoreland and she was a Graham.

Sighing, she dropped her hands to her side. "Look, don't take it personally, but I don't like you."

Chase leaned in the doorway and crossed his legs at the ankles. "Why?"

She waved her hand impatiently. "I'd think it would be obvious."

He lifted a brow. "You think we're opposites?"

She drew in an angry breath and met his gaze. "I don't know you that well, but I'd say we're as different as day and night."

Chase straightened and shot her a grin. "Then that explains it."

She narrowed an eye. "Explains what?"

"Why we're attracted to each other. Opposites attract."

Jessica snorted a breath. "I am not attracted to you!"

Chase's grin widened. "Yes, you are, and I'm attracted to you as well," he said, standing with his legs braced apart, his gaze intense, and shoulders squared.

"Believe whatever you want."

"Would you like to prove otherwise?"

She raised a questioning brow. "How?"

Chase shrugged. "Never mind, this isn't a good time to—"

"Wait! If there's a way I can prove that I'm not attracted to you then let's bring it on," she snapped.

Chase met her gaze. "Fine with me if you're sure that's what you want to do."

Jessica's shoulders were rigid with anger. "And just what is it we need to do to prove it?"

"Kiss."

At first Jessica was stunned. But then she figured it would be just like a man to want to prove anything by locking lips. Well, he would find out that she didn't enjoy kissing any more than she had making love. This was destined to be the shortest kiss on record.

She met his gaze and smiled. "Like I said, let's bring it on."

The way Chase returned her smile had her thinking that maybe, just maybe, she'd made a mistake. And when he walked past her into her shop, she had a sinking feeling in the pit of her stomach that that was definitely so.

Damn, Chase thought as he gazed at Jessica's mouth. He was going to enjoy every minute, every second that he devoured it. He bet it was as sinfully sweet and delicious as all those treats she whipped up. Sweeter.

As he continued to stare at her, pure, unadulterated lust rushed through his veins, pricked every pore of his skin and slashed waves of heat through his body. He could even go so far to say that he felt the cells in his groin reproducing.

Need propelled him from where he was standing across the room to her. He gently clasped the back of her head and pulled her closer, her lips mere inches from his. "I intend to kiss you witless," he whispered huskily.

She jutted her chin and narrowed her gaze. "You can try."

He smiled, liking her spunk. Chase hoped like hell that she put all that haughtiness into their kiss. "Open your mouth for me, sweetheart," he whispered in a deep, throaty voice.

Releasing a frustrated sigh, Jessica opened her mouth to tell him a thing or two, but with lightning speed he seized the opportunity and planted his mouth firmly on hers, silencing whatever she was about to say.

He groaned deep within his throat. His tongue thick and hot captured hers and savored it like spicy gingerbread. She had never been kissed this way before; never in her wildest imagination had she envisioned something like this happening to her.

Chase devoured her mouth like a dessert he had to have, doing passionate, provocative and illicit things to it. The man was skilled, trained, experienced and knew just what to do to make those purring sounds suddenly erupt from deep within her throat.

She couldn't believe it. With his kiss, sensual urges—

intense and strong—that she didn't recognize attacked her entire being, demanding that her body react and respond to him. She was grateful for the strong arms holding her close; otherwise she would have melted to the floor by now. She felt intense fire licking its way through her veins, her insides were simmering in heat. She was mesmerized to the point of no return.

But that's not all she felt.

His hardness, his strength, one hell of an erection was cradled between her thighs. She felt delirious, and when an involuntary shudder raced through her, she suddenly realized something. She was kissing him back. She never kissed men back. The thought overwhelmed her, overloaded her senses and sent intense heat rippling through her body.

If this didn't beat all. They had just met that day. He was a Westmoreland. She didn't like him. She didn't like kissing. She needed to breathe.

As if he'd read her last thought, he slowly released her mouth. As she stared up at him she couldn't believe they had shared something so powerful, provoking and intimate. A part of her wondered what one should say after such a stimulating encounter. But at the moment she couldn't say anything. The only thing she could think about was the way his mouth felt and how much she'd enjoyed kissing him.

"Let me go on record to say I only ended the kiss so we could breathe," he whispered, reaching up and sliding his fingers through her hair. "We might be opposites, but like I said earlier, Jessica, we do attract."

The huskiness of his words sent shivers all through

her and her skin was beginning to feel hot all over again. She could actually feel her blood sizzling. He took a step back and a warm smile tilted the corners of his lips.

"Best wishes on opening day tomorrow," he said softly.

She watched as he turned and walked out of the shop, closing the door behind him.

"I'm looking forward to working for you, Ms. Claiborne."

It had been a busy grand-opening day. The huge crowd had come and gone and they were now able to relax and take a breather. Jessica smiled at the woman, old enough to be her grandmother, and replied, "I'm looking forward to working with you, too, Mrs. Stewart. I'm just so grateful that you could help me out. I'd feel a lot better if you called me Jessica."

Delicious Cravings had officially opened at eight o'clock that morning. Jessica had been quite busy and was grateful when Ellen Stewart had walked in the shop at eleven to help with the lunch-hour traffic. But no matter how busy she'd gotten, she couldn't forget the kiss she had shared with Chase last night. It had been amazing.

Switching her thoughts elsewhere, she watched Mrs. Stewart as she dusted off the counter, thinking the woman was a huge asset to the shop with her knowledge of retail sales as well as her genuine friendliness. It seemed she knew everyone who had come in. She was a definite plus for business. But then so was Chase Westmoreland.

Most of the people who had dropped by to make a

purchase had mentioned that Chase claimed her treats were to die for. She hated admitting it, but she owed him a degree of gratitude as well, although the last thing she wanted was to owe a Westmoreland anything.

"I think it was very nice of Chase to send you customers. He's such a sweetheart."

Jessica stopped placing brownies in the display case and turned a curious gaze to Ms. Stewart. "You know Chase?"

The woman chuckled. "Of course I do. I know all the Westmorelands. Although most of the people living in Atlanta are transplants, there are still a few of us natives hanging around. I knew those Westmoreland boys and their cousins when they were in elementary school. In fact, I taught most of them."

Jessica nodded, remembering Mrs. Stewart had mentioned she had retired as a teacher over fifteen years ago. "They got into mischief like boys would do but I didn't know a more respectful group," Mrs. Stewart added. "Did you know that his brother Dare is the sheriff of College Park?"

Jessica lifted a brow. "No, I didn't know that."

"Well, he is and a good one at that. And then there's Thorn, who builds motorcycles and races them. Stone writes blockbuster books. There are also a bunch of Westmoreland cousins, like Jared, the well-known attorney. Oh, and I can't forget Storm, Chase's twin brother, although they aren't identical."

Jessica raised a brow, finding all Mrs. Stewart was telling her intriguing. "So I guess that means you know their parents as well."

Mrs. Stewart smiled warmly. "Yes. The Westmorelands are wonderful people. I knew the grandparents, too."

Jessica leaned against the counter. "Really? I understand that Chase's grandfather used to own a restaurant years ago."

Mrs. Stewart chuckled as she wiped off the counter. "Yes, and just like Chase's Place, it served the most delicious home-cooked meals around. Truckers made up the bulk of Scott Westmoreland's busy clientele, but people would come from miles around to eat his food made from secret family recipes handed down through generations. I understand Chase uses some of those same recipes and guards them like a hawk, especially after what happened when his granddad discovered that someone gave away the secret recipes to his chili, beef stew and broccoli casserole."

Jessica swallowed deeply. "How did that happen?" she asked innocently.

"I'm not sure but Scott claimed his partner, a man by the name of Carlton Graham, gave—"

"That is not true. He would not have done such a thing!"

At Jessica's strong defense of Carlton Graham, Mrs. Stewart eyed her curiously before saying, "I recall Carlton and Helen moved to California to be near their daughter and granddaughter." She lifted a curious brow. "Is there any chance Carlton Graham is a relative of yours?"

Jessica nodded, knowing there was no way she could lie to the woman. "Yes, he was my grandfather."

Mrs. Stewart's eyes widened. "Does Chase know that?"

Jessica shook his head. "No, and I don't intend to tell him until I can prove my grandfather's innocence."

"And how do you plan to do that?"

Jessica shrugged. "I'm going to start digging around in my spare time. Someone stole those recipes and deliberately made it look like my grandfather had done it. I promised my grandmother before she died that I would clear the Graham name of any wrongdoing."

Mrs. Stewart nodded. "You might want to ask Donald Schuster since it was his restaurant that ended up with the recipes."

Jessica lifted a brow. "Is he still around?"

"Yes. He's done well over the years. There's probably over a hundred Schuster's Restaurants nationwide, a few in every state, even out in California. And people claim they have the best chili around—chili some say was derived from a Westmoreland recipe."

Jessica nodded. She had heard of the chain of restaurants and had even eaten at one. "What can you tell me about Chase?"

Ms. Stewart sighed deeply. "He's a decent man who unfortunately had his heart broken years ago by a woman he met while at college. It's my understanding they met at Duke University where Chase had gotten a basketball scholarship. Everyone said that she clung to him like glue while he had a promising future in the pros. But when an injury ended any chance of that happening she dropped him like a hot potato. He's never dated another woman seriously."

The two were silent for a few moments then Ms. Stewart spoke again. "I'd like to give you a little advice if I can."

Jessica nodded. "Sure."

"Don't wait too long to tell Chase the truth about your connection to Carlton Graham. It will be better if he hears it from you than from someone else, and if you start asking questions that's bound to happen."

She leaned closer and paused a moment as if searching for words to explain. "Although all of this happened over eighteen years ago, Scott Westmoreland was deeply hurt by what he saw as an outright betrayal. In fact, he had a heart attack not long after that."

Jessica's eyes widened. She hadn't known that. "He did?"

"Yes, although I can't blame it all on stress involving the recipes. Scott was a heavy smoker and I'm sure that played a huge part in it, too, especially since he eventually died of lung cancer."

The older woman sighed deeply. "I'm not saying your granddaddy did or didn't do what the Westmorelands claim. All I'm saying is that they believe that he did it. Chase, the one closest to his grandfather, took the old man's pain and suffering personally and for years he'd tried to make Schuster admit they were preparing foods using Westmoreland recipes. Schuster refused to do so, and since there wasn't any proof, Chase eventually let the matter drop. But I doubt very seriously that he's forgotten about it."

A short while later, with only ten minutes left to closing time, Jessica was alone in her shop. She knew she had earned some pretty good profits for the first day. She sighed as she made her way over to the display case to pack up what was left of today's inventory. She had made prior arrangements with the children's hospital to donate any treats left from that day and knew someone was on their way to get them.

She couldn't help remembering what Mrs. Stewart had told her about Chase and the girl he'd fallen in love with at college. And although she hadn't wanted to feel sympathy for him, she had. The worst thing for someone to do is kick you when you're already down, and his ex-girlfriend had done just that. She hoped that over the years he had realized that he was better off without her. She wished at some point her mother had realized that she was better off without Jeff Claiborne.

She heard the tinkling of the bell on the front door, and turned, thinking it was the courier from the hospital.

Her breath caught in her throat when she saw it was Chase.

Three

"Hello, Jessica."

All day Chase had had her on his mind, and a part of him needed to see her, to see if what they had shared the day before had been reality or make-believe. And seeing her now let him know it had been real. She was as beautiful as he had remembered, everything about her was as much of a turn-on as he'd recalled.

When she continued to look at him without saying anything, he said, "I thought you probably didn't have time to eat lunch so I brought you dinner."

He watched her nervously nibble on her bottom lip and his guts clenched. "Thanks, but you didn't have to do that. I had planned to go to one of those hamburger places down the street."

He frowned. "The food at Chase's Place is tastier and better for you." He crossed the room and handed her a doggie bag. "You may want to get started on this while it's still warm."

Jessica took the bag from him and placed it on the counter. Chase was the last person she wanted to deal with right now. Seeing him here, in her shop, sent flashes of the kiss they'd shared through her mind. A part of her wanted to be angry at him for making her feel the way she did, but it was hard for her to continue to be mad at a man who went out of his way to be nice to her. And he was being nice....

She heard the tinkling of the bell on the door and turned around as a woman walked in. "Hello, I'm Gloria Miller," the woman said. "I'm here to pick up your donation for the children's hospital." She glanced over at Chase and smiled. "Hi, Chase."

"How are you, Gloria?"

"I can't complain."

Jessica couldn't help wondering if Chase knew practically everyone or everyone knew him. "I hope the children enjoy these," she said handling the woman the sealed box.

The woman grinned warmly. "I'm sure they will. Thanks for this delicious contribution." Moments later she was gone.

"That was thoughtful of you," Chase said as he glanced out the window and watched Gloria pull off.

Jessica shrugged. "No big deal. I operated on the cautious side today and baked more than I needed. I don't want to sell anything that isn't fresh tomorrow so I thought I'd donate what was left to the children's hospital."

"How will you handle the overstock inventory tomorrow?"

"I hope to bake only enough. I don't mind having a few items left but not as much as I had today. And speaking of today, I want to thank you."

Chase grinned. "You already have."

Jessica shook her head. "I'm not talking about dinner," she said. "I'm talking about all the referrals. A number of people who came in mentioned you had sent them and I appreciate the business."

He leaned against the counter. "I'm sure I wasn't the only one. The Criswell brothers dropped by for lunch and they were telling everyone about your fudge and how delicious it tasted. So they're responsible for increasing your business, too."

Jessica nodded. "I'll thank them as well when I see them." She walked over to the door after checking her watch. "It's closing time."

Chase checked his watch. "So it is."

When Chase didn't make any attempt to leave, Jessica put up the closed sign and locked the door. She also pulled down the shade to the display window, and the moment she did the interior of the shop got somewhat dark and way too intimate. "Will you get the lights, Chase?"

"In a moment."

She watched as he crossed the room, stopping directly in front of her. "Do you know what I thought about a lot today, Jessica?"

She didn't respond right away and she refused to meet his gaze. "No, what did you think about?"

He reached out and touched her chin, forcing her eyes to meet his. "The kiss we shared last night."

A part of her wanted to shout for him to get over it, but how could she expect him to when she hadn't? She had thought about it a lot that day as well. "We barely know each other, Chase. We just met yesterday. Things are moving too fast."

"You're right," he said gently, evenly. "So this is what I'd like to propose."

She lifted a brow. "What?"

"That we take the time to get to know each other."

"Why?" she asked, trying to understand. "Why should we do that?" The last thing she wanted was to become seriously romantically involved with anyone. She had a lot on her plate starting up her business. And all of her spare time was devoted to starting her investigation. The first person she intended to talk to was Donald Schuster. He was the one person who she hoped could help prove her grandfather's innocence.

"I think the answer is obvious," Chase said, interrupting her thoughts. "You don't like me. That bothers me because I don't understand why. Whenever I get within ten feet of you, I can feel your guard going up. I'm also bothered by the fact that I'm very attracted to you and I don't like being this drawn to a woman I don't really know. Hell, I didn't get much work done today for thinking about you."

"Then I suggest that you try shifting your attention elsewhere."

"I doubt if that will work. I want you."

Jessica went numb. She'd never met a man who expressed his interest in her so blatantly.

"I hope my directness didn't shock you."

She met his gaze. Yes, it had shocked her. Her heart was flip-flopping in her chest, not to mention the heat that had settled in the pit of her stomach. In California, men enjoyed playing games and you rarely knew what they were thinking, where you stood or what their intent was. "You're an attractive man, Chase, and I'm sure you date," she decided to say.

He smiled. "Not much and especially not a lot in the past six months." When she opened her mouth to continue, he pressed two fingers across her lips. "I'm not asking you to marry me, Jessica. I just want us to get to know each other. You're new in town and I'd like to show you around, introduce you to people, and spend time with you."

"You're a man. You'll eventually want more than that."

"Will I?"

"Yes." Panic gripped her. Never before had a man made her lose all sense of logic. Chase Westmoreland was powerful, dangerous and all male, and those three things had her worried.

Chase knew to tell her that she was wrong, that he wouldn't eventually want more, would be an outright lie. He glanced over at the bag sitting on her counter. "Go ahead and enjoy your food." Then, without missing a beat, he asked, "How about a movie tomorrow night?"

She blinked then stared into his eyes. He was smoothly changing the subject and they both knew it. "A movie tomorrow night?"

"Yes, a movie," he whispered, and the deep sensuous tone of his voice vibrated her nerve endings. "I'll pick you up around seven."

Her senses told her the last thing she needed to do was to begin dating a Westmoreland, but he might have some of the answers she needed. She couldn't overlook that fact. "A movie sounds nice. I'll be ready at seven." She then reached for the doorknob. "Now you can leave."

She pushed a wayward curl back from her face, inhaled and waited. His gaze was locked on hers, arousing her, making her nipples harden against her blouse. She wondered if he was aware of her body's response to him. His scent made her want to nuzzle her face into his neck and...

She closed her eyes, refusing to go there. When she slowly opened her eyes, he was there, his lips mere inches from hers. She inhaled sharply. The stir of sensual need suddenly overwhelmed her.

"You feel it like I do, Jessica," he whispered. "Don't ask me why it's happening because I don't know, but it's as if this place, this time, these moments between us were meant to be and we don't have any control over anything."

Jessica tipped her head back, refusing to look at things that way. But when he raised his fingertips to her lips, she instinctively parted them. He was right. It was as if neither of them had control over the moment. She didn't want to get romantically involved with him but a need to kiss him again was sending sensual charges all through her body. And from the way he was looking at her, she could tell he felt them.

She struggled to push down this passionate side she hadn't been aware she had. She was an ace at confrontation as an attorney, but Jessica was a novice when it came to the kind of deep-in-the-gut sensations that had her lips quivering.

"Please let me kiss you, Jessica."

With the sound of his voice, deep, husky and sexy, he didn't have to ask twice and she tilted her lips up to him. The moment their mouths connected, she swallowed a groan and let his tongue do all kinds of naughty things, pushing her pulse into overdrive and causing tingles to erupt inside her stomach. This kiss was based on more than mutual attraction and gratification. There were elements taking over that scared her to death. He was a fantastic kisser and knew he would be a great lover…but she didn't intend to sleep with him. Ever.

If only she really meant it.

She pulled back. He needed to leave. Now. "Goodbye, Chase."

He smiled. "Goodbye. I'll see you tomorrow night at seven."

And then he was gone.

The following evening Jessica breathed deeply as she crossed the room to open the door. It was exactly seven o'clock and, not surprisingly, Chase was punctual. She glanced down at herself. She had dressed casually in a pair of jeans and pullover sweater.

Jessica felt her pulse shudder when she unlocked the door to find Chase standing there. As expected, he was looking tall, dark and gorgeous. She wondered if he had any idea how he had disrupted her sleep the past two nights. "Chase."

"Jessica."

"Would you like anything to drink before we leave?" She felt another shudder pass through her when she noticed how his gaze was lingering on her mouth. A part of her wished more than anything she was immune to his robust masculinity but unfortunately she wasn't.

"No. Do you have any chocolate chip cookies left from today?"

Jessica couldn't help but smile. He sounded just like a little kid being set loose in the toy section of a department store. "Yes, I do and I remembered that they are your favorite. I've boxed them up already. You can have them when we get back."

"Oh, really…" he said as a smile spread over his face.

Jessica grinned. "Yes, really. Now are we ready to leave?"

"Let's go."

"Are you hungry?"

Jessica glanced up at Chase as they walked out of the theater. She couldn't help but chuckle. "Are you kidding? I'm the one who ate most of the popcorn, at least two hot dogs, not to mention a super-size drink and a box of gummy worms."

A corner of Chase's mouth tilted in a smile as he took her hand in his. "It's okay. I'm not a big fan of junk food."

"Umm, I can imagine. Who comes up with the menu for Chase's Place?"

"Usually I do, but Kevin gives his input."

"Kevin?"

"He's my cook but every once in a while if he's out, I do the cooking. Kevin and I are the only ones who know the Westmoreland family recipes and he's bound by a legal contract never to divulge our secrets. I had to take such measures after what happened to my grandfather years ago. He got burned putting too much trust in his partner."

Jessica swallowed the thick lump in her throat. She already knew the story, at least her grandmother's version. Now she wanted to hear Chase's. "What happened?"

"Years ago, a man by the name of Carlton Graham did most of the cooking while my grandfather handled the administrative duties. The two worked together for years and then had a dispute over something and parted ways. A few weeks later Granddad found out that Carlton had sold the secrets of a few of the Westmorelands' prize-winning recipes to a rival restaurant. Needless to say my grandfather never got over the betrayal. Those stolen recipes had been in the Westmoreland family for generations."

Jessica had to bite down on her lips to stop from coming to her grandfather's defense as she'd done with Mrs. Stewart. "And how did your grandfather know who stole the recipes?" she asked, trying not to give Chase a reason to question her interest.

By now they had reached Chase's car and he opened the door for her. "Because nobody else knew the ingredients. Also, my grandfather kept his recipe book under lock and key and no one else besides Carlton had access to it."

So of course he blamed my grandfather, she thought

as she slid into the leather seat of Chase's sports car. "What about other people who worked at your grandfather's restaurant?"

Chase shrugged. "As far as I can remember—I was only fifteen or sixteen at the time—the only other people who worked there were two waitresses, Miss Paula and Miss Darcy, and neither knew the recipes. Their job was to wait tables and take care of the customers."

Jessica nodded, thinking she had asked enough questions. The last thing she needed was for him to become suspicious.

She wished she could level with him and tell him that she was Carton Graham's granddaughter, but to do so would be a mistake until she could prove her grandfather's innocence.

Chase closed the door and walked around the car to get inside. He turned to her before starting the ignition. "You never said if you were hungry."

She shook her head and met his gaze. "No, I'm not hungry but if you are then we can stop and get you something."

He smiled. "I have an even better idea. How about if we go back to your place so I can dig into those cookies? And it would be wonderful if you have some milk. There's nothing like a big, cold glass of milk with chocolate chip cookies."

Just for a second Jessica wondered if taking Chase back to her place and inviting him inside was a good thing. But they had said they wanted to get to know each other better and she had found out some information from him tonight. On Monday she would ask Mrs.

Stewart about the waitresses who used to work for Chase's grandfather to see if they were still around. Maybe she could talk to them as well.

"Yes, I have milk and after such a wonderful evening the least I can do is take you back to my place and let you indulge your taste buds a little."

A corner of Chase's mouth tilted into a smile as he started the car. "Umm, indulge my taste buds? Now that's certainly one way of looking at it."

Four

"**I** don't think you really know how delicious these cookies are, Jessica."

Jessica leaned back in her chair and smiled, pleased with Chase's compliment. "I bet you say that to all the girls."

After taking a huge swallow of milk Chase licked his lips and smiled. "No, honestly, I don't. In fact most of the women I've dated couldn't cook worth a damn, which is probably the reason I was such an asset to them. If nothing else, I was able to feed them."

She grinned and wished she wasn't so affected by that smile of his. He had been at her place for over an hour, and during that time she had sipped her coffee while listening to him tell her about his family. She could actually feel the love he had for his siblings although he tried convincing her that his four brothers were nothing but pains.

However, he had spoken fondly about his baby sister Delaney, who would be flying into town tomorrow from the Middle East with her husband and son. A christening was planned on Sunday for his brother Storm's twin baby girls. And a christening dinner party would be held after the church service at Chase's Place.

"You've let me do a lot of talking, now it's your turn," Chase said, interrupting her thoughts.

She lifted a brow. "It's my turn?"

"Yes, tell me about yourself, Jessica."

For just a second she pressed her lips, together wondering what she could say that wouldn't lead him to make a connection to her and Carlton Graham. And if he remembered her grandfather then there was a strong possibility he would remember her grandmother as well.

She leaned forward, knowing she would have to be careful about what she said. She didn't want to deceive him but, for now, the less he knew the better. "I was born in Sacramento, California, but went to law school at UCLA and—"

"Law school? You're an attorney?"

She heard deep surprise in his voice and smiled. "I was and I guess legally I still am since I'm still licensed there. I worked for a huge corporation and was hired right out of law school. But over the years I saw just how much integrity the company lacked and often had to defend a lot of their practices that I knew were wrong."

She took a sip of her coffee, remembering those

times. "I probably would have still been there if it hadn't been for my grandmother. She died and left me an inheritance that I used to open Delicious Cravings."

Chase bit into another cookie. "What about your parents?"

"My mom was a single parent," she said quietly. "For fifteen years she believed my father would marry her, only to find out that he'd strung her along. He couldn't marry her because he was already married with a family living in Philadelphia."

She watched Chase go still. Saw the anger that came into his eyes and studied the frown that bunched his forehead. "How in the hell was he able to pull that off?" he asked.

Jessica sighed. "He was a salesman and traveled a lot. His home base was in Pennsylvania but he dropped in and paid us a visit whenever he was in town. He was able to pull off his duplicity for fifteen years because my mother never questioned his comings and goings."

She took another sip of her coffee then added, "I hated him the most when he would show up unexpectedly. My mother was a different person around him. She became weak, vulnerable and dependent. If he said *jump* she would purr, *How high?*"

Chase nodded. Although he had known Jessica only for a few days he knew she did not take after her mother. He couldn't picture any man dominating her that way. More than likely she had seen her mother live that kind of life and refused to live it herself. "How did your mom find out the truth?"

A part of Jessica wondered why she was telling him

any of this, but she knew the reason. She had discovered earlier that she felt comfortable with him. "She didn't find out. My granddad did. It had always bothered him that my father never married my mother and I guess he thought fifteen years was long enough. He also got suspicious of my father's drop-in visits and hired a private investigator who ferreted out the truth."

Chase wiped his mouth, then tossed his balled-up napkin into the garbage can that sat across the room. "How did your mother handle it when she found out the truth?" he asked, turning his attention back to her.

A shudder went through Jessica when she remembered that time. "She didn't handle it. In fact she was so devastated, so humiliated, that she overdosed on sleeping pills."

"I'm so sorry," Chase whispered and reached across the table, taking her hand in his. "That must have been awful for you."

Jessica's heart began beating wildly when Chase's hand enclosed hers. She studied his hands for a moment. They were large, strong and comforting. "It was," she said quietly. "I was fifteen and all alone except for my grandparents. I went to live with them after that. They were super and helped me through a very difficult time. Jennifer was also there for me."

"Jennifer?"

"Yes, Jennifer Claiborne, my father's legal wife. She divorced him after she found out what he'd done. Being the warm, loving and caring person that she is, she opened her arms and heart to me. She sent for me every summer so I could get to know my brother and sister and she became my second mom. She also demanded in the divorce decree that my father establish a college fund for me like he had for my sister and brother."

Chase smiled. "She sounds like one hell of a tough lady."

"She is and I know I can call on her if I ever need anything. She's always been supportive, and considering the circumstances, I think that's admirable. A lot of women would not have done all the things she did to help me put my life together after Mom died."

"What about your father?" he asked, leaning forward. Jessica's nostrils couldn't help but absorb his aftershave, which mingled with his masculine scent and was making her pulse rate escalate.

"After the divorce my father sort of dropped out of everyone's life. Last I heard he was living somewhere in New York."

"The bastard," Chase said, anger and disgust evident in his voice. "What made you decide to move to Atlanta?"

Jessica paused at his question. She couldn't tell him the real reason she had chosen Atlanta. "Mainly the cost of living. Compared to other progressive areas in the country, Atlanta gave me more for my buck and when the real estate agent located this building and said it included an apartment on top, I knew it was perfect."

She slowly pulled her hands out of his and leaned back in her chair. "I think you've eaten enough sweets for one night, Mr. Westmoreland." She glanced at her watch. "Besides that, I can sleep in late on Saturdays, but you can't."

Chase grinned. "True, but you'll need breakfast, too,

so how about joining me tomorrow? Kevin can throw down with grits and eggs."

She cocked her head and studied him. "Is that an invitation?"

"Yes, that's exactly what it is. Then if you aren't too busy you can go to a game with me around noon."

She lifted a brow? "A game?"

"Yes, I coach a basketball team of teens at the community center in College Park, and there's a game tomorrow. Chase's Crusaders against Willie's Warriors."

Jessica shook her head grinning. "Hey, I thought this was football season."

"To some people it is, but to parents who want their sons to become the Michael Jordan of tomorrow, every season is basketball season. So will you go with me?"

Jessica smiled. Although she knew she should turn him down, she said, "Basketball in October, how can I resist? By the way, who's Willie?"

Chase chuckled. "He's the coach for the other team and owns a video franchise a few blocks away. He played professionally for the Pistons a few years ago. We went to high school together and have remained good friends."

Jessica nodded. Of all the things they had talked about tonight, he hadn't mentioned anything about his dream to play for the pros. She watched him as he stood.

"Will you walk me to the door?"

"Of course."

He strolled across the room to check out her cooking pots as well as the molds that were sitting on the candy-making table. "One day you're going have to let me watch you make a batch of chocolate candy."

"Umm, maybe one day I will." She tried concentrating on what he was saying and not on what he was wearing, but there was something scrumptious about a man with wide shoulders and muscled arms in a black pullover sweater. Add a pair of denim jeans on a well-built body with firm thighs and what you got was one hell of a sexy man.

They walked together as she led him out of the kitchen to the door. Jessica tried to downplay the flutter in her stomach but couldn't, since she knew there was a good chance…a really good chance…that he would kiss her good-night. She hated admitting it but she was looking forward to his kiss.

"Breakfast in the morning?" he asked when they reached her door.

She shrugged. "Maybe. But the game is a definite."

"All right, I'll pick you up at eleven."

He leaned forward, his lips just inches from hers. "We're going to have to do something special next Wednesday," he said softly with his gaze totally transfixed on her mouth.

"Why?"

"We'll have known each other a week then." A corner of his mouth curved into a smile. "I can tell you're beginning to like me. For a while there I was worried."

They were standing so close that Jessica could feel the warmth of his breath across her face and the manly scent of him had settled firmly in her nostrils. "You want me to like you?" she asked, voluntarily scooting closer to him as he placed his hands at her waist.

"Yeah, I want you to like me. I'm a likable guy, but I can have my bad days just like anyone else."

"I'll try and remember that."

"Please do."

And then he lowered his mouth to hers. She had a pair of incredible lips and he would never get tired of kissing her. And her taste was so damn good. He wouldn't get much sleep tonight. He already knew that. So he figured he needed to remember every moment of this, every lick, every nibble, to get him through the night.

He liked the sound of her moaning. He liked the way her tongue was mating with his, and he liked the way she was sliding her hands up his shoulders. But more than anything, he loved her hot taste. He knew if he didn't stop now and pull back he would be tempted to sweep her into his arms and take her upstairs.

Moments later he broke off the kiss and whispered. "You are one hell of a woman." Jessica watched as he opened the door and walked out.

Closing and locking the door behind him, she inhaled deeply. Chase Westmoreland was as delicious as the chocolate treats she loved, but she couldn't allow herself to give in to the craving.

"You were missed at breakfast."

Jessica smiled as she stepped back to let Chase inside. As he walked into the middle of the shop with a cup of coffee in his hand, the morning sun that flowed through the display window highlighted his features and she immediately felt a sense of longing and desire.

"I decided to use my time doing something else besides eating," she said. "Win or lose I believe Chase's Crusaders deserve a treat so I spent the morning baking cookies."

Evidently surprised, he cocked his head and stared at her. "You did?"

She grinned. "Yes, I did. I figured it was the least I could do to contribute to such a worthy cause. I think it's wonderful that you're taking the time to spend with them."

Chase shrugged. "It's no big deal. They are a wonderful group of kids. Besides, I love basketball. It was my dream to play in the pros but an injury stopped me. So I finished college and came back here."

She nodded. "That's when you decided to open your restaurant?"

He smiled and leaned against the counter. "No, that idea didn't come until three years later. Like you, I got a job in corporate America, working as a financial adviser. It didn't take me long to get fed up with office politics and make a career change."

He laughed. "Believe it or not, the idea for opening a restaurant came from my brothers. I'm the one who spent the most time with my grandfather when he was in business. I worked at his restaurant after school and on weekends. So I was the one who he passed all the family recipe secrets to. And since I loved to cook, my brothers—who were all single at the time—usually ended up at my place for dinner, so they suggested I go into business for myself."

He took a sip of his coffee, then added, "I had some money saved, my brothers chipped in and we found the building I'm in now. At first it was a family affair where everyone pitched in and worked, even my parents. But when I started seeing a profit I figured that I could afford to hire paid help."

"And now Chase's Place is a popular hot spot known for its mouth-wateringly delicious soul food," Jessica said, remembering something Mrs. Stewart had told her earlier in the week.

His smile widened. "Yes, and I'm very proud of that."

"You should be. Have you given any thought to franchising?"

"Yes, especially lately. But I have to be certain that the warm, friendly, family atmosphere I've worked so hard to achieve won't get lost."

He glanced at his watch. "Are you ready?"

She smiled. "Yes, I just need help getting the box of cookies out to your car."

She moved across the room to go into the kitchen, and he placed his cup on the counter and intercepted her. She glanced up at him and immediately felt a flutter in her stomach. Warning flags went up—as they had last night—signaling her that they were moving too fast; it was too soon and that she shouldn't get involved with him. He was a Westmoreland—the enemy. But whenever he looked at her the way he was doing now, the last thing she wanted to dwell on was bad blood between their families.

"Let's make plans for next week," he whispered, as one corner of his mouth tilted into a smile.

"What kind of plans?" she found herself asking.

"Dinner at my place Wednesday night around eight."

She lifted a brow. "But I thought you closed early on Wednesday. At six."

His mouth curved even more. "I do. A lot of people around here go to prayer meetings at their church which usually include dinner. But I just happen to know the owner of Chase's Place and he's given me permission to bring a special guest after hours."

She chuckled. "Oh, he did, did he?"

"Yes, he did."

Again, warning flags were flapping around in her head, but at that moment she chose to ignore them and said, "I'd love to have dinner with you Wednesday night."

"Thank you."

And then he leaned down and kissed her.

"We were totally surprised when Chase mentioned he had invited someone to today's game," Tara West-moreland, the wife of Chase's brother Thorn, said smiling. "And we think it's wonderful."

Jessica was confused. "Why would you think that?" she asked. When she and Chase had arrived at the community center he had taken her to a group of four women. Three he had introduced as his sisters-in-laws—Shelly, Madison and Tara; the other was his cousin Jared's wife, Dana.

It was Shelly, Dare's wife, who answered. "Because Chase is a very private person and he's never brought a date to any of the games before."

Jessica shrugged as she leaned back on one of the bleachers. The game would be starting in less than ten minutes. "I'm not really his date. We met this week when I opened a confectionery a few doors down from his restaurant. I moved here from California, and since

I don't know anyone in town he was kind enough to invite me along today."

Madison, who was married to Stone, grinned as she patted Jessica's hand. "Trust me, he never would have brought you over to us if you weren't his date. Chase guards his privacy like a hawk." The other three women agreed and nodded knowingly.

Jessica blinked, not sure what to think. She didn't want anyone assuming that she and Chase were involved. They weren't. She glanced down at the basketball court and saw Chase talking to his brothers and cousins. Anyone who saw the group of men would know they were related. She had met the Westmoreland men earlier and found them to be nice, likeable people, although she hadn't wanted them to be.

On the car ride over, Chase had surprised her by inviting her to his nieces' christening as well as the dinner party he planned to host afterwards at his restaurant tomorrow. To include her in such an important family affair was a bit too much and she had declined. Besides, she had made plans to meet with Donald Schuster tomorrow. She had called him yesterday and he had agreed to meet with her at his home.

"Chase's looking this way again," Tara said grinning. "Smile for Chase, Jessica, so he'll know you're okay and aren't suffering from our company."

Jessica couldn't help but smile. These Westmoreland women were too much. She really liked them. She met Chase's gaze and smiled. He smiled back before directing his attention back to the group of youngsters on his team.

"Don't look now but here come the guys," Dana said, smiling, seeing her husband and his cousins climbing the bleachers toward them.

"They will be as curious about you as we were," Shelly whispered to Jessica grinning.

Jessica shot the women a nervous look. "Surely they aren't going to ask me anything about my relationship with Chase?"

Tara chuckled. "No, they're depending on us to pump you for information and later they'll corner us and expect us to come clean and divulge everything that we know."

"But don't be surprised if Dare asks you questions," Shelly added, grinning. "It's the cop in him so don't take it personally. Besides, he's the oldest of his brothers and is somewhat protective, although he'll never admit it." She leaned back in the bleachers and shook her head and chuckled. "And now that he sees how taken Chase is with you, he's bound to get downright nosy."

Jessica stared at the women, not sure if they were serious. It didn't take long for her to realize they were. She swallowed, thinking the last thing she needed was Sheriff Dare Westmoreland asking her a lot of questions.

By the time the Westmoreland men had reached them she had tried to contain her nervousness.

"So, where are you from, Jessica?" Dare asked, not missing a beat as he eased into the spot next to Shelly.

Jessica forced a smile. "Sacramento. Have you ever been there?"

"Yes, for a law enforcement convention a few years back. It's a nice area," he responded.

"Yes, it is a nice area," she agreed.

"Why did you leave?"

Jessica knew everyone was waiting for her answer. She wasn't one to get rattled easily, but Dare Westmoreland was doing a good job of shaking her composure. It wasn't that he was outright rude in his questioning, but she hated being placed in a situation where she had to explain herself to anyone. But in this case she would. It was obvious that the Westmorelands were a close-knit group and a part of her envied the care and concern that they had for each other.

"Job stress," she finally said, leaning back on the bleacher and tucking a strand of hair behind her ear. "I was an attorney in a—"

"You're an attorney?" Jared cut her off by asking.

Her gaze moved from Dare to Jared who she knew was the attorney in the Westmoreland family. She smiled when everyone fell silent. "Yes. I went to law school at UCLA and then went to work for a large corporation. Starting off I loved my job but over the years I discovered just how much the company lacked integrity and more than once I found myself defending practices that I knew were wrong."

"So you walked away?"

Her gaze moved from Jared to Tara and felt a sense of relief at the look of admiration in her the other woman's eyes. "Yes, but not before I had what I considered a workable plan. My grandmother passed and left me an inheritance, so I decided to use it to fulfill my dream of opening my own business. I've always enjoyed baking with chocolate and I decided a change in areas and careers was what I needed."

"Why Atlanta?"

Breath held, Jessica shifted her gaze from Tara back to Dare. There was something in his dark-brown eyes that made her wonder if he suspected that there was a lot more than what she was sharing with them. She forced herself to hold his gaze while saying, "I knew someone who used to live here and remembered her saying how nice it was. Besides, everyone knows this is a city on the move. There's something for everyone."

Dare opened his mouth to ask her another question but before he could get the words out, the buzzer sounded, indicating the start of the game. Everyone's attention shifted from her to the activities on the court below. Jessica let out a silent sigh and started to relax somewhat, but then she noticed Dare was still studying her curiously and knew she would have to stay on her guard around him.

"You have to be proud that your team won," Jessica said hours later as she and Chase walked out to his car. After the game the parents had served refreshments. Her delicious baked treats had been a big hit.

"Yes, I am. I think the guys did a good job. They showed good teamwork and that's what's most important, the team and not individual egos. If we can instill that mindset into them now, they'll be better athletes if and when they make it to the pros."

He glanced at his watch. "My sister Delaney and her family should have arrived by now and everyone will be over at my parents' place. Would you like to go over there with me for a while?"

Jessica inhaled deeply. She had enjoyed herself with the Westmorelands at the game today but the last thing she wanted was to continue to give them the impression that she and Chase were an item. "Thanks for the invite, but I think I'm going to turn in early tonight. This has been one busy week for me. The grand opening was great but tiring, and I want to spend the rest of today and tomorrow relaxing."

"All right." He looped an arm around her shoulders as they continued walking toward his car. Chase, Jessica was discovering, was a very nice person and she didn't want to think about what his reaction would be when he found out she hadn't told him everything about herself. But for now, she couldn't. Until she could come to him with proof of her grandfather's innocence, the less he knew the better.

Five

As Jessica drove through the security gate that led to the Schuster estates, she was glad Donald Schuster had agreed to see her. After telling her that he had remembered her grandfather, no doubt he was curious about what she wanted.

As she approached the huge ranch-style home set on what had to be at least four acres of land, she couldn't help but think how quickly she could prove her grandfather's innocence if Mr. Schuster were to tell her who had given him the Westmoreland secret recipes. Then she could present her findings to the Westmorelands and proceed with her life as she had planned. If nothing else, this week had shown her that people wanted a pastry shop in the area and more than once she had been approached with the idea of supplying pastries for neighboring businesses.

Moments later Jessica found herself knocking on a huge wooden door and blinked when a butler dressed in a starched uniform answered. "May I help you, Miss?"

She smiled. "Yes, I'm Jessica Claiborne and I'm here to see Mr. Schuster."

The butler nodded. "He's expecting you."

The butler led the way, and Jessica followed, glancing around at the extravagant surroundings. Everything she saw said *money,* but there was something about the place that reminded her of a museum more than a home.

She stopped when the butler paused and opened a door that led out onto a glassed, enclosed patio. An older man, who would have been close to her grandfather's age had he lived, was sitting in a wheelchair looking out over a huge lake.

"Mr. Schuster, your guest has arrived," the butler announced.

The man immediately turned the wheelchair around to look at her. A smile touched his aged face. "Come in," he said in a strong voice. He offered her a chair across from him. "You said you wanted to ask me questions about your grandfather and that episode with the Westmoreland secret recipes."

Jessica nodded. "Everyone thinks my grandfather is the one who gave them to you."

The man waved a frail hand in the air. "No one gave me anything. Although some of my entrées may have tasted like Westmorelands' they weren't. I tried to tell Scott Westmoreland that, but he was too bullheaded to listen, and I guess it didn't help matters that he knew I'd been trying to convince your grandfather to become my partner. But there was this friendship thing between him and Westmoreland and nothing would shake that."

Jessica was saved from saying anything when the butler brought in a tray of iced tea. When she found herself alone with Mr. Schuster again, she said, "Evidently something did shake their friendship, since he stopped working with Scott Westmoreland."

"Yes, but he would have eventually gone back. The two got into it all the time but they would always resolve their disagreements and get back together. They made a hell of a team. Your grandfather was a great cook and Scott, bless his stubborn hide, was one hell of an entrepreneur. And I understand his grandson Chase Westmoreland is just like him. He's a fantastic chef and has a good head for business when it comes to running a restaurant."

Jessica smiled, thinking that the older man had paid Chase a nice compliment. "And you're sure there's no way you were using any of the Westmoreland recipes?"

The older man chuckled. "At my age I wouldn't bet my life on anything, but my cook at the time said they were was his own recipes, and I had no reason not to believe him."

Jessica nodded again. "Could you tell me his name?"

"Theodore Henry. But we called him Teddy for short."

"Does he still work for you?"

"Heavens no, he stopped working for me years ago. But I understand Teddy owns a catering company in town."

Jessica took a huge sip of her tea then set the glass down and smiled. "Thanks, Mr. Schuster, you've been a big help and I appreciate you taking the time to see me. I intend to find Mr. Henry and talk to him."

"Hey, Chase, will you quit looking out that window? Jessica hasn't returned yet. If I didn't know better I'd think you were really smitten with her."

Chase turned and frowned at his brother. "I just met her a few days ago, Thorn."

Thorn shrugged, smiling smugly. "So? All it took was a couple of seconds for Tara to knock me off my feet."

Better than her knocking the hell out of you. Chase shook his head, reminiscing. He could vividly recall the night Tara and Thorn had met. Tara had been so mad at Thorn he was lucky she hadn't whacked him. "No one is knocking me off my feet," he finally said.

"If you say so."

Chase inhaled deeply. Sometimes he wished he'd been born an only child.

"Dare thinks there's something suspicious about her," Thorn added.

Chase raised his eyes heavenward. "Dare's a cop. He thinks there's something suspicious about everyone."

Thorn chuckled. "That's true. I don't think he was too happy that she was so close-mouthed about herself and her family."

Chase leaned against a table, remembering what Jessica had shared with him the other night. It wasn't exactly something he'd want to share with the whole world if it had happened to him. He'd felt touched that she had told him as much as she had. "She's a private person, Thorn. Let it go."

Thorn smiled. "Hey, it doesn't bother me if your woman has secrets."

"She's not my woman."

"Who isn't your woman?" their sister Delaney came up and asked.

"The chocolate chip lady," Thorn said grinning. "She makes the best damn chocolate chip cookies."

Chase narrowed his eyes. "She made them for the guys on the team, but I couldn't help noticing that you, Stone and Dare grabbed a few."

Thorn shrugged. "They looked too tasty to pass up and they reminded me of the cookies Grampa's cook used to bake before they went their separate ways years ago. And as far as your team goes, all that sugar in a teenager's mouth isn't good. Think of all the cavities. We did their parents a favor."

Chase was about to say something when he noticed Jessica's car pulling into the parking lot.

"Looks like your woman is back," Thorn said as a smile tilted a corner of his mouth.

Chase shrugged nonchalantly. "So? What of it?"

Thorn rubbed his chin. "That's what I'm wondering myself," he said as he walked out of the room.

It was close to five o'clock by the time Chase had tidied up his restaurant and taken out the last of the trash. His brothers had hung around to help, but he was glad when they'd finally left. They had ribbed him enough for one weekend.

He locked the door to his restaurant and glanced over at Jessica's place wondering what she was doing. She'd said she would spend the weekend relaxing and he didn't want to bother her, but a part of him had to see her.

What he had told Thorn was true. He and Jessica had known each other for only a few days. But he had to admit that in such a short length of time he had learned more about her than he had about some women he'd dated for a full month. He'd learned about all the unhappiness she'd had in her life and how much she enjoyed baking. He liked talking to her and felt comfortable telling her about the injury that had kept him from going to the pros. But he hadn't mentioned anything to her about Iris and the broken heart she had dealt him during that time.

He smiled when he thought of the hit Jessica had been with the kids on his team and their parents. Everyone had appreciated her thoughtfulness in wanting to reward the team with goodies. There hadn't been a shy bone in her body while interacting with everyone, including his family. He liked the way she smiled when she found something amusing, but he also thought her frown was absolutely adorable. During the short time they had known each other, he had told her more about himself than he had shared with any woman before.

But how could he trust her, or any woman? After the episode with Iris, trust wasn't something that came easily with him, especially when it involved a woman. He was a private person, reluctant to talk about his personal business and he pretty much kept things to himself. He did share a close bond with his brothers and cousins, and once in a while he would talk to them about things that were important to him but never about women. No woman had ever gotten close enough to him again to cause that type of grief. They came into his life and they went out of his life. That's the way he wanted it and that's the way he intended to keep it.

So why was he becoming obsessed with Jessica Claiborne?

He strolled over to his car to leave, and just as he was about to unlock the door he paused. Inhaling deeply he turned and began walking toward Jessica's shop. With every step he took he tried to convince himself that he was just being neighborly by checking in on her. He didn't have to go inside. He would just say hello and leave.

But moments later, when she opened the door, all thoughts of leaving suddenly left his mind. It was obvious that she had recently showered. And that she wasn't wearing a bra under her tank top. He blinked, not wanting to stare. She had great-looking breasts. They looked full, firm and lush pressed against the soft fabric of her top. Damn, he shouldn't be looking at her breasts. He wished he could do more than just look at them. Tasting them wasn't such a bad idea right about now.

He tore his gaze away from her chest and his eyes moved downward. She was wearing shorts that showed off her gorgeous legs and he suddenly felt his attraction for her get sharper, more intense.

He should be avoiding Jessica like the plague. Their relationship was not what his brothers assumed. But still, he was man enough to admit that there was a flicker of forbidden desire that clenched his guts whenever he saw her, came this close to her. Why was he putting himself through such madness? He sucked in a deep breath and smelled her scent—like cinnamon, spice, every-thing sensual and everything nice.

"Chase?"

He heard his name and then remembered he was standing there and hadn't said anything. "May I come in?" he finally asked.

Her legs somewhat shaky, Jessica met Chase's stare. Getting rid of him would be easy enough. All she had to do was refuse his request to come in. But for some reason she didn't want to. She tried to tell herself that this intense attraction between them had gone on long enough and it was time to take drastic action. Telling him that she was Carlton Graham's granddaughter would guarantee that he would walk away for sure, but she wasn't ready for that to happen. She couldn't tell him who she was until she could also prove her grand-father's innocence.

She sighed deeply and took a step back. When he was inside with the door closed behind him, she saw the heated look of desire in his eyes. Her first instinct was to run, head up the stairs, but she had a feeling he would only come after her. So she might as well stay put and get something they both wanted. For someone who didn't like kissing, she was becoming obsessed with doing it. Her mouth had practically been branded Chase's Place.

Jessica made a move toward Chase, as if drawn by a magnet. At the same time, Chase moved closer to her. "This is crazy," she said in a breathless whisper as she walked into his arms.

"Yeah, totally insane," he said huskily, pulling her closer to him.

She tilted her face up, and he did what was becoming as natural as breathing; he captured her mouth with his, blazing the heat already sizzling between them, satisfying their need to taste each other.

Kissing him got better each time. He had that special technique of letting his tongue sweep the corners of her lips, first sipping her gently like fine wine before deepening the kiss and sucking her tongue into complete submission, mating wildly with it and driving her insane. Only with Chase could she allow herself to open fully and take part in such an intimate exchange. He had the ability to arouse feelings that she wanted to explore. She wasn't able to do anything but stand there, hold on and shudder in his arms.

Moments later, he pulled back, reached out, palmed her face in his hand and brushed a kiss over her forehead. "I wanted to check on you to make sure you were okay." Then, knowing that was really a lame excuse, he added, "And more than anything, I wanted to taste you again."

Giving in to this uncontrollable desire, he leaned closer and kissed her mouth again, wishing he could kiss her forever. He finally lifted his head and their gazes met. And he knew what they had agreed on earlier was true. This was crazy. But that didn't stop him from kissing her again before he finally left.

She never was good at counting sheep, Jessica thought a few hours later as she lay in her bed gazing up at the ceiling. Who could think of sheep when thoughts of Chase Westmoreland filled her mind?

The taste of him was still fresh in her mouth, and she didn't want to think about the feel of him. Her breath was coming out in short gasps just thinking about the size of the erection that had been cradled between her thighs as he had continued to kiss her deeper and deeper.

She'd known she could have pulled back to stop him at any time but she hadn't wanted him to stop. So he hadn't, until it became obvious that if they continued she would have found herself on the floor with her shorts off, legs spread, and Chase naked between them. After kissing her into sweet oblivion, he had told her that he hoped she slept well tonight then left.

Jessica wasn't sleeping at all. She snapped her eyes shut. Instead of a flock of sheep flooding her mind, she saw Chase as she had seen him earlier that night, just moments before he'd left. He had been standing in her shop, gazing at her with so much desire in his eyes.

She almost jumped when she heard the phone ring and quickly reached over to pick it up while glancing over at the clock. She smiled and sat upright in bed. How could she have forgotten the call she got around this time every Sunday night?

"Hello."

"Hello, Jess, how did things go?"

Jessica's smile widened upon hearing Jennifer's voice. "The grand opening was wonderful."

"Sorry I missed it."

"Trust me, I understand." And she did. Jennifer Claiborne had been appointed school superintendent in Philadelphia, and since the school year had only started a month ago, she hadn't been able to get away.

"Have you heard anything from Savannah lately?" Jessica asked about her sister who was a year older and worked mostly out of the country as a photographer.

"Yes, she called today and said she had tried contacting you, but you weren't home. And she couldn't reach you on your cell phone. Of course she didn't leave a message. You know how she hates talking into those answering machines. I also talked to Rico today and he said to let you know he'll be in your area next week and plans to stop by."

Jessica grinned. "And I'm going to look forward to his visit," she said. Rico was four years older, a private investigator and she simply adored him.

She and Jennifer talked for over an hour. She told her about the information she had gathered to prove her grandfather's innocence.

"And you're sure Chase Westmoreland doesn't have a clue who you are?" Jennifer asked for the second time.

"Yes, I'm sure. He knows me as Claiborne so there's no way he could make the connection." That was the way she wanted things until she was able to tell him everything.

"Well, I hope you're not making a mistake by not telling him the truth up front."

Jessica shook her head. "He's a Westmoreland. He wouldn't trust me. Like his grandfather didn't trust my grandfather."

"It also seems to me from what you've told me about him that he's a nice guy. Possibly someone you could become interested in."

Too easily, Jessica thought, remembering the intense attraction she and Chase shared. "You know how I feel about having a serious relationship, Jennifer."

"Yes, and like you I have reasons to feel that way, but there's a need within all of us to be loved by someone."

Jessica sighed. Until she had met Chase she would have denied that such a need existed, but now…

"I'd better let you go. I'm sure you have a big week ahead of you."

After hanging up the phone, Jessica shifted to a more comfortable position in bed. She couldn't dismiss another type of need trying to take over her mind and body. It was a need she had never experienced before, but one she always encountered whenever she and Chase kissed. It was the need to take things further and enter into a scorching affair with him, based on need, not love, something she had never done before. She wasn't sure if she could handle it. And if she couldn't stand the heat, she should probably just stay out of the kitchen altogether.

Six

"So you remember the two waitresses who used to work for Chase's grandfather?" Jessica asked Mrs. Stewart while restocking the display case with fudge.

"Paula Meyers and Darcy Evans? I sure do," Mrs. Stewart said smiling. "Paula still lives in College Park but Darcy moved to Macon a few years ago to be closer to her family."

"And what about Theodore Henry? Mr. Schuster's former cook?"

"Yes, I knew him, too. He was a single man, nice-looking, soft-spoken, pretty much kept to himself. He rarely went to church, but he didn't bother anybody. He did what he had to do at Schuster's and minded his own business."

Jessica nodded. She intended to speak to Mr. Henry and Paula Meyers by the end of the week. Getting together with Darcy Evans might take longer since she would have to drive to Macon to do so.

She preferred speaking to everyone in person. From her days as an attorney she learned that face-to-face communication was much more effective than discussing anything over the telephone.

Hours later, after Mrs. Stewart left for the day, Jessica found herself alone in her shop as she tried to decide what would be tomorrow's craving of the day. But the only craving she could think about was the one she had for Chase. She couldn't erase from her mind the enjoyment she got kissing him. It didn't take much for her to remember the gentle yet thorough sweep of his tongue inside her mouth, assailing her senses with every stroke, and how he would feast on her lips. He had the ability to dismantle each and every wall she erected around herself.

And that wasn't good.

She glanced at the clock. She had an hour left before closing time. When Donna, the waitress from Chase's restaurant, had dropped in earlier to buy some brownies, she had casually mentioned that Chase had to leave town unexpectedly for Knoxville, something about a screwup in one of his deliveries, and that he wouldn't be back until Wednesday.

Jessica had accepted Donna's statement with a small shrug, which she hoped indicated her indifference. But the truth of the matter was she wasn't indifferent. How could she be when the thought that she wouldn't be seeing Chase again until Wednesday made her miss him already?

They were supposed to have dinner at his restaurant—after hours—to celebrate a week of knowing each other. He wasn't interested in anything other than enjoying a good wholesome time with a woman, based on friendship and nothing else. Okay, so they did throw a lot of kissing into the mix, she thought. But still their relationship was based on friendship, although that might crumble when he found out her true identity.

She sighed when she heard the phone ring and reached to pick it up. "Delicious Cravings."

"Yes, I'm returning a call to Jessica Graham. This is Paula Meyers."

Jessica smiled. "Yes, Ms. Meyers. Thanks for returning my call."

"Are you sure there won't be anything else, Chase?"

Chase glanced up from looking at the invoice. He was eager to leave Knoxville and head home but it seemed that Sam Nesbitt's daughter was on the prowl again. Storm had dated Cyndi once and now, with Storm happily married, it was obvious that she had shifted her attention to his single brother. "I'm positive. Looks like everything is in order."

"I would definitely agree," she said, giving him a thorough once-over while licking her lips.

Seeing her lick her lips did absolutely nothing for him. If it had been Jessica's lips, there'd be no way he would have been able to downplay the thrill and excitement that would have rushed through him.

"I'm about to close shop, Chase. I know a place where we can go and…get it on."

Chase lifted a brow. Storm had warned him that Cyndi Nesbitt didn't mince words or waste time. She spoke her mind and told you exactly what she wanted, and most of the time she could get pretty damn graphic. As he gazed at her, he knew she could probably deliver on her offer of recreational sex. But the fact of the matter was he wasn't interested. The only woman he wanted was back in Atlanta.

Placing a polite smile on his face, he said, "Thanks for the offer but I have a few more stops to make before returning to Atlanta sometime tomorrow. Tell your father that I'm sorry I missed him."

A disappointed pout curved her lips. "Yeah, I'll be sure to tell him."

Later that evening Chase was back at his hotel. After taking a shower he lay on the bed and found his mind filled with thoughts of Jessica. Inexplicable warmth flowed through his bloodstream. He had never met anyone quite like her. He shifted his body and rubbed the back of his neck. Okay, he knew he shouldn't be thinking about her so much, but the blind truth was that he couldn't help himself. It was nothing more than a sexual attraction fueled by six months of him doing without, but still, there was something about Jessica that drew him, made it impossible for him to want any other woman but her.

He leaned forward and picked up the business card he had placed on the nightstand earlier, the card Jessica had given him on Saturday for Delicious Cravings.

Sighing deeply, he picked up the phone and began dialing. When it began to ring he glanced at his watch. It was close to eight o'clock and he hoped he wouldn't be disturbing her.

"Hello?"

At the sound of her sweet voice he released a long, deep breath. The warmth flowing through his bloodstream increased as he settled back against a huge fluffy pillow. "Hi, Jessica. It's Chase."

Jessica curled her body as she lay on the bed and a heated sensation flowed through her stomach. She took a deep breath. The sound of Chase's voice was doing things to her. "Chase, how are you?"

"A whole lot better now that I'm talking to you."

A thrill shot through Jessica at his words. He definitely knew how to break through a girl's defenses. "I had to leave this morning on an unexpected trip to Knoxville," he was saying, reclaiming her attention. "I've been having problems with my suppliers and I thought a face-to-face meeting was warranted."

Jessica nodded. "I've heard that Knoxville is a beautiful city."

"It is. I gather that you've never been here."

She smiled. "No, I haven't."

"Then I'll have to invite you to come with me the next time I make a trip this way."

Chase murmured the words low, in a deep, husky tone. His breath seemed to transcend the phone lines and warmly caress her ear, heating the flesh along her spine. His invitation wasn't helping matters. "I'd like that." She ignored the warning bells sounding in her ears. She and Chase were moving a little too fast, but she didn't see them slowing down any.

"So, how was your day?" he asked.

She didn't want to think of her meeting that afternoon with Paula Meyers. The older, sweet and seemingly gentle woman hadn't been able to tell her anything about who might have passed the Westmoreland secret recipes on to the cook at Schuster's restaurant. Jessica would be taking a drive to Macon to talk to Darcy Evans the next afternoon. When she had called, the woman hadn't seem too excited to talk with her.

"Today was wonderful," she said. "Business was good. In fact I got another contract to supply pastries for a nearby hotel."

"Sounds like you're doing well. But then, I knew that you would."

When Jessica tried uncurling her body, heat ran down her spine again. "Thanks." A few moments into the conversation she asked, "So when will you be coming home?"

"Sometime Wednesday. You haven't forgotten about our dinner plans, have you?"

She took a deep breath, not wanting to tell him that she hadn't thought of much else. Even the disappointing dead end with Paula Meyers hadn't dampened her thoughts of sharing a meal with Chase on Wednesday night. "No, I haven't forgotten. I'm looking forward to it," she said truthfully.

"So am I." After a few moments he said, "I'm sure

you've had a busy day and need your rest so I'll let you go. Good night, Jessica."

She hated that their phone conversation was coming to an end. "Good night, Chase, and thanks for calling."

After hanging up, Jessica traced the lines of her lips with her fingertips, remembering the time it had been Chase's tongue and not her finger caressing her lips. The memory sent an arousing shiver through her. As she stretched out in bed she could hear the steady tap of rain beating down on her roof.

Cuddling her pillow she shifted her body into a comfortable position knowing that the moment she closed her eyes, thoughts of Chase would consume her, even while she slept.

Darcy Evans was hiding something.

Jessica could feel it. The woman, who appeared to be in her mid-thirties, said she had only agreed to talk with Jessica because of the respect she'd had for Jessica's grandfather. Eighteen years ago she had been a seventeen-year-old unwed mother in need of a job and Carlton Graham had talked Scott Westmoreland into hiring her as a waitress. She hadn't worked there long when Scott and Carlton parted ways.

"So you have no idea how the Westmoreland recipes could have gotten into the hands of the cook at Schuster's restaurant?"

Jessica watched the expression on the woman's face. As she stood leaning her hips against the closed door, she replied, "How would I know something like that? I was just a waitress."

Yes, how indeed? Jessica wondered as she continued looking at the woman. "And you were a waitress there for a couple of months?"

"For four months actually."

"And during that time you never worked in the kitchen?"

The woman's eyes flared. "And just what are you accusing me of?"

Jessica sighed. "I'm not accusing you of anything, Ms. Evans. I'm just trying to find answers to an unsolved puzzle."

The woman lifted her chin. "Why bother? Scott Westmoreland and Carlton Graham are dead. What does it matter what happened with those recipes?"

Jessica picked up her purse and stood. "Because although they've passed away, their descendants deserve to know the truth, and until they do, my grandfather's honesty will be questioned. That's unfair to him. I want to prove he wasn't guilty of any wrongdoing."

Jessica watched the woman tense up and look around the small apartment as if not wanting to meet Jessica's eyes. "Your grandfather was a good man."

Jessica smiled. "Yes, I think so, too, but he died knowing there was a blemish on his character and that always bothered him. And I'm asking that if you remember anything that you think might help clear his name, will you please let me know."

"I won't remember anything," Darcy Evans said, much too quickly, Jessica thought as she was ushered out the door.

* * *

Chase turned and glanced around the room. His office had been transformed into a place he almost didn't recognize. While in the kitchen preparing the dinner he would share tonight with Jessica, he had given Donna instructions on how he had wanted things set up, and it appeared his ever-efficient waitress had gone overboard. The way she had changed a section of his office into an intimate dining area for two definitely met with his satisfaction, but what was up with the lit fireplace and all the flowers and candles? There was no way he could dine in here with Jessica and not think of seduction. He would want to kiss her, take her upstairs to the small apartment he used on occasion, and undress her. Then he would run his hands all over her breasts, stomach and thighs, not to mention touch that area between her legs that had definitely become his own delicious craving. He felt a tightening in his loins. He wanted to do more than touch her there. He wanted to taste her, devour her and watch her eyes fill with the pleasure he was dying to give her as she opened her legs wider and his tongue continued to—

"Everything meets with your satisfaction, boss?"

Jerked out of his racy thoughts, Chase turned and met Donna's excited features. He sighed. "You kind of went overboard, don't you think?"

Donna chuckled. "Well, considering how things went the first time Jessica Claiborne walked into your office, I figured you needed all the help you could get, and I have a feeling that she likes to be wined and dined like the rest of us."

Chase nodded as he studied the woman he had hired six months ago. Donna had become someone he could depend on. Although he didn't know a lot about her personal life since she kept that pretty private, he did know that she was twenty-three and was attending school at night to earn a degree in business management.

A few hours later when he was alone Chase's primitive instincts kicked into gear. His staff had cleaned everything up and left for the day. He hadn't seen Jessica since Sunday and although he had spoken to her on Monday night from Knoxville, he had talked himself out of calling her again on Tuesday. He had convinced himself that his desire for her was natural and he would just have to ignore the low burning need that always simmered in his gut whenever he was around her. Tonight the two of them would celebrate a week of knowing each other, although he didn't want to dwell on the fact that he'd never commemorated a week of knowing any other woman.

He sighed, almost impatient to see her again, to kiss her, talk to her, then frowned, wondering what the hell was wrong with him. He didn't have long to ponder that question when he heard a knock at the door.

Ignoring the racing of his heart, Chase opened the door and for a moment just stood there staring at the woman standing in front of him. She was dressed in a skirt and blouse that would have looked simple on any other woman. The outfit did a pretty nice job of emphasizing her full, firm breasts, tiny waist and curvy hips. And, he thought, glancing downward to take a look at her legs, which could easily be seen thanks to the shortness of her skirt, there was definitely temptation there, especially with the high-heeled sandals she wore. Her scent, hot and seductive, also triggered something within him. Like he wasn't heated up enough already.

He didn't say anything for a moment and watched as she nervously swept her bottom lip with her tongue. Pure unadulterated lust hit him with the force of Mount St. Helens erupting.

"I hope I'm not too early, Chase," she said softly, glancing up at him.

His gaze came to rest on her mouth when he said, "No, you're right on time." And I want to taste you bad.

He took a step back, let her in, then closed and locked the door behind her. The air surrounding them seemed to quiver and the need to take her into his arms and kiss her was slithering through every vein in his body.

"I thought I'd contribute dessert," she said, handing a covered container to him. "Chocolate cheesecake."

"Thanks." He slowly felt his control slipping and knew he had to get a grip. Grip, hell! He placed the cake container on a nearby table and reached out and pulled her into his arms. As soon as his lips captured hers he knew kissing her was becoming an addiction. It should be against the law for any woman's mouth to taste this sweet, this delicious, this able to whet his sexual appetite.

He hadn't known how much he needed this until now. He needed to bury his mouth in hers, suck her tongue, feel her breasts pressed against his chest, and hear the way she moaned when he kissed her. And then there was the way her body automatically connected to his groin, fitting his arousal dead center between her thighs—the part of her he craved most.

Damn if he didn't put a stop to this madness, he would be taking her right here, right now. Slowly, reluctantly, he lifted his head and almost drowned in the heated look in her eyes. "I thought it would be best if we dined in my office," he whispered against her moist lips. "That way no one would see the lights on in here and assume I'm open for business." In other words, he didn't want any interruptions.

"All right."

He suddenly felt warm again and he inhaled deeply, trying not to focus on her mouth. Trying to pull himself together, Chase picked up the cake container off the table and placing a hand at the center of her back, he led her down the hall. Neither said a word. When they reached his office door he pushed it open and watched as she walked into the room.

Her gaze immediately went to the table set for two, the lit fireplace and the flowers and candles. She didn't say anything for a moment, turning slowly. The eyes that met his were like a soft caress and did nothing to cool his desire, only heightened it.

A smile tilted the corner of her mouth when she said, "You didn't have to go to all this trouble, Chase."

Yes, I did, he thought, as he slowly strolled toward her, covering the distance separating them. He placed the cake container on his desk and to keep from reaching out and touching her, he tightened his hands into fists at his side.

The way her hair tumbled around her shoulders,

made her look sexier than ever, and now, within the close confines of his office, her scent, a delicious fragrance that was the very essence of her, further ignited that primal instinct already playing havoc with every part of his body. Kissing her earlier definitely hadn't helped matters.

"I hope you enjoy dinner. It's a Westmoreland secret recipe for chicken and dumplings."

Jessica swallowed. The last thing she wanted to hear anything about was a Westmoreland secret recipe. "Is it good?"

He chuckled. "I'll let you decide." He walked over and pulled out a chair at the table. "Come and let me serve you."

She nodded and sat down at the table. Jessica watched as he expertly served the food, struggling to remain calm and fighting not to stare at him. She hadn't realized until now just how much she had missed him these past couple of days. Nor had she realized how much she had needed him to kiss her. He had such a dark, handsome, sophisticated look, yet her senses told her that there was a hint of something untamed about him.

"Let's dig in," he said after they'd said grace.

During dinner they talked about a number of things. He even gave her pointers on how to promote her business on the Internet. Afterwards, they savored the cheesecake she had brought.

"Did you enjoy dinner?" he asked softly sometime later, when they stood in front of the fireplace enjoying a glass of wine.

She smiled. "Yes, I enjoyed everything. The chicken and dumplings were to die for."

She glanced around the room at the flowers and candles then turned back and looked at him. "Everything was nice, Chase, but I'm wondering…"

When she hesitated and didn't finish what she was about to say, he asked, "Wondering what?"

She nervously bit her bottom lip. "I'm wondering if perhaps it's a little too much for two people who've decided to be just friends."

Chase had crouched down in front of the fireplace to add another piece of wood to the flames. He lifted a dark brow and glanced at Jessica. "When did we decide that? We talked about things moving too fast and slowing them down a bit. We also agreed to take the time to know each other better. But I don't recall saying we wouldn't be anything more than friends. In fact I'm counting on just the opposite. I don't want to be only your friend."

He studied her as he stood, watching every nuance of her features as the words he'd spoken sank in. "What are you saying?" she whispered softly, her voice the only sound in the room other than the resonance of the fire crackling in the fireplace.

He sighed, knowing he had to give her the bare truth. No frills, no gimmicks, no lies and definitely no game-playing. He wanted to be her lover and not her friend. Usually he didn't move this fast with any woman, but with Jessica he was driven to do so. "We've already discussed the issue of us being attracted to each other. But there seems to be another problem, a deeper one."

Her brows furrowed in a frown. "What?" She tried to downplay the churning in her stomach as he looked at her. His dark eyes, shadowed by long lashes, were doing things to her.

His features were serious when he said, "I want you, Jessica, and I think you want me as well. We can do whatever we want to skirt around that fact, avoid it or ignore it, but eventually the final result will be the same."

She lifted a brow. "The final result?"

"Yes."

"Which is?"

"We *will* become lovers. If not tonight, then some other night. The chemistry between us is too strong for us not to. I would never force or trick you. But I will try my best to seduce you."

Seduce you...Chase's words flowed through her mind and as much as she didn't want them to, they stirred a sensual need in her. They did more than that, they ignited something deep and elemental. She turned to study the flames in the fireplace, but they were nothing compared to the ones inching through her bloodstream at that very moment.

For two solid days she had tried keeping her mind focused on finding out how Schuster's cook had gotten hold of the Westmoreland secret recipes, but Chase had always lurked deeply in her thoughts.

She heard him come to stand behind her. She breathed his masculine scent, and knew that what he'd said was true. Considering their families' history, an involvement with him was the last thing she needed. But he was right. Sooner or later they *would* sleep together, even though she hadn't liked sex in the past. She knew that with Chase things would be different. He'd already changed her mind about kissing.

"Jessica?"

He whispered her name just moments before he reached out and gently turned her around. Dark-brown eyes studied her intently, searching her face, heating her insides and melting her resistance. For longer than she cared to remember, she had been an independent woman, placing no aspect of her life or livelihood into a man's hands. But then those hands had never belonged to Chase Westmoreland.

The truth of the matter was that she wanted his hands to hold her, snuggle her close to him, touch her all over, give her the pleasure she had dreamed he had given her just last night. Just thinking about it made her pulse fierce, her breathing erratic, her heart beat wildly and generated an intense amount of heat between her legs. She drew in a shaky breath knowing what she was going through was more than mere lust, but at the moment she didn't want to define anything.

She struggled against the need to be sensible versus her desire to be wanton. There was a heart-beat of a pause, and then she reached out and wrapped her arms around Chase's neck and brought her body against the hard solid plane of his. She felt how aroused he was through his slacks and the intense sexual need she had been fighting since first meeting him took control.

"Chase," she murmured softly, deciding to throw

caution to the wind and take what she wanted for the first time in her life.

"Yes?"

"Seduce me."

Seven

Seduce me…

Jessica's words sent Chase's libido into overdrive. He gazed at her, thinking that not only did he plan to seduce her, he intended to drive her wild. "Will you join me in another glass of wine?" he asked quietly against her ear.

She nodded as a shiver passed through her, uncertain of his plans for her. But whatever they were she would be a willing participant. She met his gaze and held on to it. "Yes."

Emotions were churning inside her as she watched him pour them each another glass of wine. "I propose a toast," he said huskily, gazing at her with those dark penetrating eyes that had her body simmering. "To seduction."

Jessica let her gaze shift from him to stare at the hand holding his wineglass in midair. This wasn't the first time she had studied his hands and wondered how they would feel on her. Even now, just thinking about it had her senses overheating. She swallowed deeply as she clicked her glass to his then slowly drank her wine. When she had taken a couple of sips he reached out and gently eased the glass from her hand and placed it beside his on the table. He turned to a CD player that sat nearby and after he had turned a knob, soft jazz filled the air.

"Let's dance," he whispered, pulling her into his arms.

Jessica could feel her body tremble from the hardness of his pressed intimately to hers. She gave in to the seductive moment surrounding them and closed her eyes as the soft sound of the music lulled her, sharpened her feminine instincts. She nestled her face against his throat, breathing in his manly, arousing scent. The light stroke of his fingers on her back inched lower, past her waist to caress her backside. His touch was driving her insane, making her want things she'd never had. Molten heat filled her entire body.

More than once her pelvis pressed into him; she was fully aware of his erection, large and thick, and she was surprised by her ability to make him want her that much. He splayed the palm of his hand inside her buttocks, bringing her closer to him, making her breathing shallow and the area between her legs even more damp.

All too quickly, the song ended. She glanced up and met his gaze. She saw the heated look in his eyes, noted the raw primitive expression on his face mere seconds before he leaned down to connect his lips to hers. Hands that she had been studying earlier reached out and cradled her head, delving into her scalp, as he mated his mouth with hers, slowly, easily, thoroughly.

Then he deepened the kiss, sucking her tongue into his mouth, letting her know just how much he wanted everything he could get and driving her mad in the process. He ground his aroused body against hers and she groaned as he continued to kiss her with a passion that had liquid heat flowing between her legs, making her want him there. *Oh, yes, right there.*

She felt his fingers inching up her leg, moving slowly, toward her inner thigh and the feel of him touching her made her suck in a quick breath. He pulled back, releasing her mouth and the look he gave her was so incredibly sexy it made a deep quivering need invade her insides.

"I think you have on too many clothes," he whispered as he reached out and began unbuttoning her blouse. "I want you naked." He continued to hold her gaze. "Do you have a problem with that?" he asked softly as he eased the buttons out of the buttonholes.

She reached out and held fast to his arm. Not to stop him but to hurry him along. His slowness was almost killing her. "No, I don't have a problem with it," she whispered, reveling in the warmth of his skin beneath her fingers.

When the last of the buttons had been undone and he saw her flesh-colored lace bra, he inhaled sharply. His hands went first to the front fastener and, with a quick flick of the wrist, her bra came undone and her breasts sprang free.

Jessica heard the deep sound of male appreciation that erupted in his throat and her stomach clenched at the way he was staring at her breasts. There was hunger in his eyes. She held her breath as he eased the bra from her shoulders, letting it join her blouse on the floor.

"I've wanted you from the first day I saw you. It wasn't here in this office. It was before then. That Monday morning I saw you move into your place," he whispered. "The first thing I thought was that you had a gorgeous pair of legs," he said smiling wryly. Then his features turned serious when he added, "Gorgeous legs or not, I didn't want to get involved with you, but I soon discovered I could do nothing to stop it from happening."

He breathed in deeply. "I want you so much," he groaned just moments before leaning down and capturing one of her nipples with his mouth.

Jessica sucked in a deep breath when his mouth connected to her turgid nipple, licking at it, sucking it into his mouth and lavishing it with the warmth of his tongue. He was assaulting her emotions to the third degree, causing a purr to erupt deep within her throat, making her legs give way.

As her knees buckled, he brought her body closer to his, holding her up, not letting her go anywhere while his mouth switched breasts, tormenting the other as he had its twin.

"Chase." Jessica moaned his name on a soft sigh as her hand reached out to hold fast to his head, not wanting him to stop what he was doing to her. He was filling her with passion to a degree she'd never known could exist.

He pulled back. "I want to taste you some more," he whispered throatily, holding her gaze, making the ache within her even more profound.

She inhaled sharply and to her amazement she heard herself say, "Then do it."

The smile he gave her melted her insides and destroyed any resistance that might have suddenly popped into her mind. She watched as he undid her skirt to let it slide down her legs and pool at her feet, leaving her wearing nothing but a pair of flesh lacy thong panties.

"Sexy as hell," she heard him growl in a deep, rough tone before going on his knees and gently easing her panties down. Then he leaned back and looked up at her, letting his gaze roam all over her. His eyes came back to the area between her legs. When she saw him lick his lips she knew what was coming next. She had heard about it, read about it, but had never experienced it herself. In a few moments she would. Chase would make sure of it.

He eased closer to her and leaned over and placed a kiss on her navel, licking the area around it, making it wet then blowing warm air on it, making the heated warmth between her legs intensify. She watched him as a flush of desire surged through her.

He slowly made his way downward, past her navel, and before she could catch her next breath he was kissing her there with the same intensity that he had applied to her mouth. And to make sure she wasn't going anywhere—like she would even consider such a thing—he placed a firm grip on her buttocks, holding her still while igniting her entire body into flames.

She heard the guttural growls he was making as he kissed her and, of their own accord, her hands clutched his head. He sank farther into her warmth, deepening the kiss and tasting her in a way no man had ever done before.

With a groan, she thrust her hips closer—as if his mouth wasn't planted in place firmly already—but what she wanted was for the waves that were insistently pounding at her insides to finally drown her. It was evident that Chase would not be rushed. He intended to feast on her until he got his fill, until his hunger to taste her this way was assuaged.

But her body suddenly exploded and she screamed his name. She tried pushing him away from her, but he gripped her buttocks tighter, firmly locked his mouth to her as his tongue moved inside her wildly, uninhibitedly, stroking her, tasting her thoroughly. He didn't release his grip until the last tremble had left her body, and then he didn't stop what he was doing, but continued to taste her as his hands gently stroked her hips.

Finally, he lifted his head, eased back on his haunches and looked at her. The look in his eyes made her breath catch. He wanted more. A lot more. And as she watched him lean forward and nuzzle his face in the area between her thighs, heaven help her but she wanted more, too. "Make love to me, Chase," she whispered.

He pulled back, looked up at her, eased to his feet and then swept her into his arms.

Chase gazed down at the woman he was holding. Usually he wouldn't do what he had just done until he

got to know the woman better, but Jessica was a decadent delicacy and he couldn't have resisted sampling her
that way even if he had wanted to. And now that he had
tasted her, his craving had intensified. She was utterly
delicious.

He held her tenderly while walking up the stairs and
couldn't help but notice how she cuddled in his arms,
rubbed her cheek against his chest, causing his breathing to quicken, his libido to go into overdrive.

When he reached the bedroom he drew in a deep breath,
crossed the room to the bed and lowered Jessica. He had
felt her heat the moment she had walked into Chase's
Place tonight, and now he wanted to get all into it again.
But first he had to get as naked as she was. Looking at her
lying there on his bed without a stitch of clothing was making him lose control of all coherent thought. Tasting her
was nice, definitely a mouthwatering experience, but what
he wanted to do more than anything was get inside her.

As he stood back to unbutton his shirt, he watched
her watching him. The moonlight streaming in through
the windows bathed her in a translucent glow, making
the coloring of her body as luscious as the chocolate she
used to bake with. "Say something," he whispered when
the quiet stillness in the room got unbearable and it was
obvious what he was doing had her complete attention.
He tossed his shirt aside.

He watched as she stretched her naked body while a
smile touched the corners of her lips. He liked the fact
she wasn't shy or bashful. Nor was she ashamed of
showing her body to him. She laughed quietly, sexily.
"What do you want me to say?"

Heat flooded his brain when she took her tongue and licked her lips. He swallowed the lump in his throat as his hands went to his belt buckle. "You can say anything."

She paused, as if taking in his words, and when she licked her lips again he sucked in a quick breath. He watched as she eased to the edge of the bed, her face coming in direct contact with his midsection. She reached out and pressed her hand against the large, heavy erection clearly showing through his slacks, using her fingers to explore the firmness of it through the khaki material. "Umm, at the moment, I can think of only one word to say," she said softly and in a voice he found incredibly sexy.

"What's that?" he asked, barely able to get the words out as she continued to explore him, squeeze him, cup him.

She lifted her gaze to meet his and with a deep, throaty sound she said, "Hurry."

He smiled as he took a step back and quickly pulled the belt from his pants before easing both his underwear and slacks down his legs. He stood before her as naked as she was and got heated watching her eyes roam over him. "What are you thinking?" he asked in a strained voice.

"What I thought the first time I saw you. That you remind me of rich dark chocolate," she whispered. "And that I would definitely like to have some of it."

He chuckled and slowly moved toward the bed. "Baby, I intend for you to have all of it."

He joined her on the bed, urging her back to the middle of the mattress. Without wasting any time he pinned her body beneath his weight. "But first," he said, leaning in and bringing his face down to hers, "I need to kiss you again."

Jessica smiled. She knew all about his kisses, was well aware of how delicious and X-rated they were. Ever since meeting Chase she had become aware of the extent of the sexual desire she had stored away, denying its existence. Before she could ponder why, his mouth captured hers, making her forget everything but the way he was working his tongue inside her mouth. Memories of what he had done to her while on his knees in his office, along with what he was doing to her now, sent sensuous shudders all through her, tumbling her emotions and getting her body overheated.

When he finally released her mouth, he whispered quietly, so incredibly sexily in her ear, "Open for me, Jessica."

Instinctively she spread her legs as he continued stroking his tongue back and forth across her lips. She felt him lift his lower body and she unconsciously lifted hers. "Now take me in," he whispered hoarsely.

He leaned up and met her gaze and she knew what he was asking her to do, which was something she'd never done—lead a man into her body. But she would do it. She wanted to do it. Before, when she had made love that one time in college, things had been over before she could blink, leaving her feeling cheated, unsatisfied, disappointed. But Chase was making sure she was a part of what they were doing. He was allowing her to be more than a willing partner. He fully intended her to be an eager participant.

Reaching out she came into contact with the hairy

surface around his navel. Her fingers paused, liking the feel of the rough texture of hair there on his stomach. When her fingertips began caressing him there, she heard his sharp intake of breath.

"Jessica."

Her name was a tortured groan from his lips and she smiled as her fingers moved downward until she got hold of him. He felt hard, firm, big in her hands. She blinked. *Too big*. She wondered if they would fit.

She glanced up and met his gaze. As if knowing her thoughts he smiled and said, "Perfectly."

She breathed in deeply, deciding to take his word for it. Besides, holding him in her hand was making her lose control of all rational thought. The only thing she could think about was that the huge, thick object she was clutching would soon be inside her, mating with her and…

She blinked again. "What about protection?" she suddenly asked.

She could tell from the expression on his face that he had forgotten just as she had. He sucked in a deep breath. "Damn, I'm usually not this careless. Sorry," he said, shifting his body off her to retrieve a condom packet from the nightstand drawer. He ripped it open with his teeth and quickly sheathed himself.

She smiled, although she still wondered how they would fit. "I sort of got carried away with the moment, too." She paused, then quickly added, "I'm on the pill to regulate my periods but I haven't slept with anyone for over eight years—"

"Eight years?" A shocked look took over his features.

She nodded. "Yes, not since my first year at college.

It wasn't anything like I thought it would be and was over quickly." A part of Jessica couldn't believe she was discussing this with Chase as if they were having a conversation about the weather.

"And you haven't done it again since then?"

Jessica swallowed before answering. "No, this will be the first time since then."

Returning to her, he bent his head, took her lips, dipped his tongue into her mouth, kissing her with such gentle tenderness Jessica thought she would faint. Then he deepened the kiss, reigniting the flame between them, causing her body to ache for him once again.

"Lead me in, Jessica," he said moments later, breaking off their kiss.

His breathing was choppy and his whispered words made her entire body pulse. Holding him firmly in her hand, she guided him to her as their eyes met and held. The intensity in his gaze sent heat throbbing through her. She actually felt the muscles in her womb contract. It seemed that every part of her was ready to receive him.

When he was at her entrance she felt him take over. The tip of him eased inside, stretching her, and as he lowered his hips and she lifted hers, he went deeper. She sucked in a deep breath when he couldn't go any farther.

Chase raised up slightly and gazed down at her. "You're still… He didn't…" He broke off in amazement. He leaned down, his face mere inches from hers.

Before Jessica could fully understand what Chase meant by those words, she felt him push his body forward, and the cry of pain that tore from her lips was captured in his kiss. She'd been a virgin all this time. He continued kissing her and she couldn't recall a more precious moment.

Instinctively, she wrapped her legs around Chase's waist as he continued kissing her. Moments later, he pulled back and whispered, "Make love with me, sweetheart."

Her legs tightened around him. Her body was coiled with anticipation of what was next. And when he pushed deeper inside her, locking them legs to legs, limbs to limbs, breasts to chest, she lifted her hips to him.

He began to move. Slow at first, driving her almost insane with the way his body was moving in and out of hers. Then suddenly his strokes quickened and they mated effortlessly, smoothly, fluidly. His hips slammed into her over and over again. As if that wasn't close enough, he took his hand and lifted her and she thought she felt him touch the crest of her womb.

"Chase." She cried out his name, begging for a release that was different from the one she'd had earlier in his office. Different but just as intense. His tongue inside her had been awesome, but his sex inside her, pumping into her fast, solid, hard, was even better. Over and over he continued, nonstop. Every single thrust brought her closer to the edge. She wanted to scream, her throat ached to do so.

And she did.

She screamed his name. Her arms circled his neck and felt all the perspiration that soaked his skin. Sweat trickled down his back, slicked his forehead, and dampened her flesh. But he didn't let up and she cried out again, everything inside her exploding—including him.

She heard his guttural cry just moments before she

felt the warmth of his release. He was not holding anything back, determined to make her shatter, break free, blast off to the stars, detonate into ecstasy. And he was there with her, grinding his teeth, pushing deeper inside her as both of them continued to come apart. He relentlessly pounded into her hard and fast, and she felt his second release, just as intense and thick as the first. His head fell back and he screamed her name as explosions continued to erupt between them.

And Jessica knew at that moment that as unbelievable as it might seem, she had fallen in love with Chase Westmoreland.

Chase's body shuddered as he eased off Jessica. They had made love a second time and he'd have liked nothing better than to pin her body under his and go another round. He doubted if he would ever tire of making love to her.

His delicious craving. He'd never known a woman so damn edible.

He glanced over at her. He'd worn her out. She could barely keep her eyes open. After the first time they had made love he had gone into the bathroom. When she had seen him standing at the foot of the bed with the basin of water and wash cloth, she had drawn back and looked at him as though he'd lost his mind, not believing he would even for one minute consider performing such an intimate act on her. She had tried being stubborn about it, but in the end he had kissed her into submission. He had never slept with a virgin before. Even Iris had been experienced.

He inhaled sharply when he thought of the woman

who had wounded his pride and broken his heart. When he had been at the top of his game, at the head of the list for the NBA draft, she had been right there, on his arm and in his bed. But after his injury she hadn't wasted time moving on to bigger opportunities and even had the gall to tell him that it wasn't anything personal, but she wanted more from life than to be tied to a cripple. That had been nearly ten years ago. He no longer walked with a limp thanks to the extensive physical therapy he had endured, a very supportive family and the willpower and determination to survive as well as to succeed.

He glanced back over at Jessica and saw she had drifted off to sleep. But still he heard her murmur his name as she shifted in bed and wiggled her bottom to fit into him. His physical reaction to her cradled so snugly against him was immediate. His craving for her absolute. He splayed his palm on her stomach and gently pressed her closer to him, spooning their bodies, and he heard when she murmured his name again.

Chase frowned slightly. The last thing he needed at this point in his life was another woman getting under his skin. Once burned, it was hard not to wear a shield. He had made the decision long ago never to fall in love again. Doing so would only be asking for pain. For that reason he was troubled by his deep attraction to Jessica. Even before they had shared what they had tonight, he had been entranced by her, which wasn't a good thing. When it came to women he wasn't into attachments.

He glanced at the clock on the nightstand. It was a little past midnight. He would need to wake her before four o'clock to make sure she got dressed to return to her apartment. Some of his employees began arriving around five to handle the early-morning breakfast crowd. The last thing he wanted was for anyone to know his and Jessica's business. As far as he was concerned, what they'd shared was too precious for prying eyes at the moment. Everyone would discover sooner or later that they were having an affair, but he wished it to be later and not sooner.

Chase cursed under his breath when he thought about his brothers and cousins. They would try making a mountain out of a molehill but at that moment, Jessica shifted again in bed, bringing her bottom even closer to the fit of his front, and his brothers and cousins were the last thought on his mind.

Jessica slowly opened her eyes and felt a strong, warm arm slung across her waist. A very naked waist. It suddenly occurred to her that she was completely naked and so was the man lying so close beside her in the softly illuminated bedroom.

She peeked at the clock on the bedside table. It was three o'clock in the morning. She felt her pulse quicken at the memory of what she and Chase had shared last night, and all because of Chase's very talented mouth. She closed her eyes as heat flowed through her.

Then something else rushed through her as well. The stark memory that she had been a virgin. Chase was now the first for her in a lot of ways. The first man to give her a climax and the first man to actually make love to her in the full sense of the word. There had been nothing quick about it and the last thing she felt was cheated.

Jessica felt her face burn with embarrassment when she also remembered what he'd done after they had made love the first time, and the gentle, attentive care he had given her afterward. She had never imagined any man being that caring and concerned with a woman he'd slept with. Just thinking about what he had done to soothe her aches would endear him to her for life. And when they had made love a second time, he had been so gentle and tender it had almost brought tears to her eyes.

A sharp pain stabbed at Jessica's heart when she imagined what Chase's reaction would be when he discovered she was Carlton Graham's granddaughter. She knew Mrs. Stewart and Jennifer were right. She should tell him the truth and continue to go about proving her grandfather's innocence. From just the short time she'd gotten to know Chase, she felt that trust was an important issue to him.

Suddenly, Jessica's breath caught in her throat when she felt his arm shift from her waist as his hand moved slowly downward, toward the juncture of her legs.

"Sore?" he asked, his voice warm and soft, as he brushed his lips across an area beneath her ear.

Jessica opened her mouth to answer but she let out a soft purr instead when his fingers began caressing her feminine core, making scorching heat swirl inside her. She swallowed deeply and then tried to speak again. "Not too much, thanks to you." She felt the moistness of his tongue as he licked an area against her neck. She immediately gasped for air.

"No thanks needed."

In one smooth move he had rolled her from her side

onto her back and she found herself trapped intimately beneath his hard, solid body. The eyes staring down at her were sexy as sin. And immediately she felt the heat simmering within her ignite, flame out of control. Right now, at this very moment, she wanted him to make love to her again. She needed it. Later she would rake herself over the coals for falling in love with him, but for now…

She raised her arms to encircle his neck, bringing his mouth down closer to hers. "Make love to me again," she whispered, meeting the deep intensity in his gaze.

Although she might be the one making the request, she knew that he wanted her just as much as she wanted him. The proof was there in the thick, hard, turgid erection resting so achingly close between her thighs. But she knew that Chase was the kind of man who wouldn't make a move until she'd given him permission to give her pleasure.

And then, slowly, she began to feel him inch his way inside of her. The dark eyes she was gazing up into became even darker. Her body automatically stretched as he went deeper, and flicks of intense heat began consuming her.

"I love being inside you," he growled in her ear, and she wrapped her legs securely around him, locking their bodies as his shaft inched deeper still. When he had gone as deep as he could go, he leaned down and when her lips parted on a low, breathless moan, he claimed her mouth, at the same time as the lower part of his body began moving in deep, penetrating thrusts, over and over again.

And then it happened. Pleasure slammed into her and she was stunned by it. She had reached a climax with him before, but this one almost jerked her body clear off the bed, made her arch desperately against him, and felt as if she was coming apart, fragmenting into a million pieces. Chase lifted his mouth from hers to throw back his head and a deep howl filled the air as he experienced his own pleasure. As if she wasn't close enough, his hands cupped her bottom to bring her closer so he could go deeper, fusing their bodies as one.

Then his lips covered hers and he took her mouth with a promise of more fulfillment as exploding waves drowned them once again, sweeping them off to a place where it seemed their souls had somehow melded.

Before dawn that morning Chase opened the door of his restaurant to walk Jessica home. The air was cool and everything was quiet and still.

He automatically placed his arms around her shoulders and brought her body close to his as they strolled in the darkness passed Mrs. Morrison's shop. No words were exchanged between them and Chase wondered if Jessica felt the way he did, that what they'd shared was a dream and one uttered word would bring them awake.

When they reached her door he watched as she unlocked it. She turned back to him and Chase quickly leaned down and pressed a kiss upon her lips. He wondered how one ended what had turned out to be such a very special night. And if she were to invite him in, how would he turn down her invitation when more than anything he wanted to make love to her again—for the rest of the morning and the remainder of the day as well?

The kiss that he had meant to be short and sweet suddenly took on a life of its own, and he found himself kissing her deeply, with abandoned possession and simmering hunger. He knew he should pull away from her, but decided he couldn't imagine having his mouth in any other place at the moment.

Finally, when they heard the loud horn of a semi-truck somewhere in the distance, they moved apart. She met his gaze and he could see the same desire he felt mirrored in her eyes.

"I'd better go inside," she whispered softly. "And thanks again for dinner."

Chase smiled. "Thank you for *everything*."

Jessica's stomach clenched. She both loved him and wanted him. A deadly combination. Without thinking what she was doing she leaned up on tiptoes and brought her lips to his. He took the kiss she offered, added his own little sensual twist.

She slowly pulled back. "Good night, Chase."

A broad grin touched both corners of his lips. "And good morning to you, Jessica." He turned and then walked away.

Eight

The first thing Chase noticed when he walked into Jessica's shop at lunchtime was the slew of customers lined up at the counter that had yet to be waited on. And it appeared she was trying to work the lunchtime crowd all by herself. He wondered aloud where Mrs. Stewart was.

Jessica had glanced up when she heard the sound of his voice. She met his gaze and smiled.

"She called in. She wasn't feeling well and was determined to come in anyway, but I talked her into staying home."

Chase lifted a brow. "And you're trying to handle this crowd all by yourself?"

"Yes."

Before she could blink, he had come behind the

counter and snagged an apron off the rack. He then put on a pair of food-handler's gloves. Jessica turned and stared at him. "What are you doing?"

He smiled at her. "Helping out."

"B-but…"

He turned her back around. "You have a customer, Jessica. Don't keep Mrs. Prescott waiting. If I'm not mistaken this is her day of beauty and she can't be late at the salon."

The older woman who was standing on the other side of the counter beamed. "That's right, Chase. And Harry and I will be at your place for Friday's night's special. I'm counting on it being fried chicken, collard greens and potato salad."

Chase chuckled. "And just for you and Mr. Prescott, I'll make sure that it is."

Mrs. Prescott then turned to Jessica. "And don't put up a fuss about him helping out, young lady. I've known those Westmoreland boys since the day they were born. The last thing you have to worry about is one of them robbing you blind."

Jessica couldn't help but smile. That *was* the last thing she was concerned about. But how would she be able to do anything with Chase so close? There wasn't much space behind the counter and she didn't know how she and Chase would share it. She and Ms. Stewart were two relatively petite women, but Chase…well, Chase was well-built, muscular, had a nice set of abs, not to mention a few other qualities she considered outstanding. She'd been an eyewitness to those qualities just last night, and the memory made heat rush into her face.

"Hey, you okay?" Chase leaned over and asked her, almost too close for comfort.

She blinked and tried to control her rapid heartbeat. "Yes, I'm okay." *If you call thinking about last night okay.* "Why you ask?"

He chuckled. "Because Mrs. Prescott has been trying to give you her money for the past couple of minutes."

"Oh." Jessica turned to the older woman apologetically. "I'm sorry."

The older woman smiled. "That's okay, I understand. I used to be young once."

Jessica swallowed. Had the woman picked up on her attraction to Chase? She was more than ready for the next customer, determined to keep her concentration on her customers and not on Chase. A few moments later she discovered they worked well together. He knew just what her customers wanted and even talked them into buying something extra. For the next hour and a half they had a steady flow of customers, but by two o'clock the store was completely empty.

Jessica glanced over at Chase as he removed his gloves. "Thanks for the help. You're good for business," she said smiling.

"Umm, I hope I'm good for more than just business," he said grinning suggestively as he removed his apron and hung it back on the rack.

Jessica shook her head and chuckled. "Trust me, you are."

His grin widened. "That's good to know."

Jessica sighed. She had meant every word of what she'd said. Memories of their time together last night had kept her pretty heated much of the day. One thing the busy lunch hour had done was keep her mind occupied and off him…until he had shown up unexpectedly with his offer to help.

Chase glanced down at his watch. "I'd better go before everyone wonders where I took off to." He chuckled then said, "But then I think they'll know if Luanne Coleman has her way."

Jessica raised a brow. "Luanne Coleman?"

"Yes, the woman who was in here wearing the red dress and straw hat."

Jessica nodded, remembering. "Was she the one who held up the line for ten minutes trying to decide whether she wanted a batch of brownies or fudge and didn't make up her mind until you gave her a sample of each?"

Chase laughed. "Yes, that's the one. She and her husband own a flower shop in College Park and she is the town's biggest gossip. It's my guess that after she left here she went right over to the restaurant and spread the word that I was helping you out."

Jessica stared at Chase. "But why would that interest her?"

Chase leaned back against the counter. "The last I heard Mrs. Coleman and the other older ladies in her sewing club are betting on the next Westmoreland to get married."

"The next Westmoreland to get married?"

"Yes. Some are putting their money on me and some on my cousins Ian and Durango." At her confused look Chase chuckled again and decided to explain. "My brothers and cousins and I haven't ever wanted marriage in our future but within the past three years, all of my brothers have gotten married."

"Oh."

"Then a few months ago my cousin Jared surprised all of us by getting engaged. He and Dana got married, so quite naturally everyone turned their eyes on me since I'm the last of my brothers. Although I've told them many times I'd never marry, they don't believe me."

Jessica nodded. "And why not?"

"Because my brothers and Jared always said the same thing—that they would never marry. And although I would be the first to admit that they're all happy, it means nothing to me. The bottom line is that I'll never marry."

Jessica turned away from him, pretending to be absorbed in wiping down the glass case. She didn't want him to see how his words affected her. She may have fallen deeply in love with him, but that was her problem, not his. She had a feeling he was deliberately emphasizing something he'd said last night. She had heard him loud and clear when he'd said he was into casual relationships. A man into casual relationships didn't have marriage on his mind. She was smart enough to know that. Maybe it was time she let him know her position as well. "I never intend to get married either," she said as she wiped off the counter. She didn't look up but felt his probing eyes on her anyway.

"Why not?"

Jessica decided to look at him since he actually sounded confused. "I told you the story behind my father, Chase. What he did affected my ability to trust. Not that I think all men are the scum of the earth like he was, but I pretty much decided I have more to do with my time than worry about whether the man I'm with is trustworthy."

Chase nodded. "Yes, I know what you mean."

Jessica met his stare. "Do you?"

Chase fell silent for a moment then said, "Yes. I do. I got burned in college when the woman I thought loved me dropped me like a hot potato when my injury kept me from playing pro ball."

There was a pause and then he added, "I was quite bitter for a while but soon wised up and decided I was better off without Iris. Still, that hasn't stopped me from being cautious. I'll never trust another woman with my heart again. Trust is important to me. I can't stand deceit of any kind."

She nodded slowly, not wanting to consider the fact that at that moment she was deceiving him. "Umm, so I guess we understand each other."

Chase was quiet. Then he said, "Yes, I guess we do." He looked back at his watch again. "I'd better go." He then looked at her and asked. "What are you doing later?"

"I'm going out."

He raised his brow. "Out?"

"Yes." She decided she didn't owe him any further explanation than that. The last thing she wanted him to know was that she intended to pay a visit to Theodore Henry. The man had refused to return her calls. She had heard from Mrs. Stewart that he would be catering a fund-raising dinner in East Point, a suburb of Atlanta, tonight. She intended to show up and talk to him whether he wanted to talk to her or not.

"How about taking a two hour drive with me to Chattanooga on Saturday?"

"Chattanooga?"

Chase smiled. "Yes. I'm going there to pick up motorcycle parts as a favor to Thorn. He's busy building a bike for his next race."

Jessica thought about his invitation. She had never been to Chattanooga before and had always heard how beautiful the city was. Although she knew the best thing to do was not get more involved with Chase than she already was, the bottom line was she couldn't help it. She wanted to spend time with him. "I'd love to go to Chattanooga with you Saturday."

His smile widened. "Great. I'll pick you up Saturday morning around eight. Is that a good time for you?"

"Yes, that's a perfect time, and I'll be ready."

For a long moment neither of them said anything, but they stared long and hard at each other. And, as she gazed into his dark eyes, Jessica could feel the heat beginning to rise between them. She wondered what Chase was thinking when he tipped his head back and continued to stare at her. Was he remembering last night in his office and then later in his bedroom? She had enough memories stored for the both of them. Even now, with him standing there, she could vividly remember him kneeling between her thighs and the swirl of his tongue as he greedily devoured her.

She felt her stomach clench and her thighs actually trembled at the memory. As if he'd read her thoughts—was tuned right in to what she was thinking—he took a couple of steps toward her when the bell on the door sounded. A man walked in.

Chase inhaled deeply as he watched as Jessica turned to greet the customer. His entire body felt tight, wound-up, hot. It was as if he'd read her mind and had gotten caught up in her sensuous thoughts, her candid memories of the time they had spent together last night.

Pulling in another deep breath, he watched as a huge smile touched her lips before she raced from behind the counter to be engulfed in the man's arms.

"Rico!"

Chase frowned. Who the hell was Rico? And judging from the gigantic smile on Jessica's lips she definitely knew the guy. Was this the guy she was going out with later? Suddenly, without much glamour or fanfare, an emotion he hadn't experience in a long time attacked his insides. He didn't know who the man was, but he wanted to cross the room and snatch Jessica out of his arms.

He made a move, then caught himself, astounded that he would feel that way. Not since Iris had he felt jealousy for any woman. Fighting for control he leaned back against the counter. Okay, so he usually wasn't the jealous type, but dammit, at the moment he was seeing red.

"Maybe I should leave," he said in a somewhat angry voice.

Two pair of eyes shifted to glance over at him. Evidently the extent of his anger registered. He saw a sparkle in the man's eyes. In Jessica's he saw clear confusion. Hell, he was confused about the way he was acting as well.

"Umm, maybe you *should* leave," the man named

Rico said, smiling, although the smile didn't quite reach his eyes.

Chase's frown deepened. He straightened, suddenly filled with a desire go over and smack the man, break the pretty boy's nose.

"Rico, stop," Jessica said, chuckling. She met Chase's hard stare and the smile vanished from her lips. She wondered what had him so upset. Then it dawned on her. She had told him she was going out later today and then Rico showed up. She couldn't help but smile again at the possibility that he was jealous.

She shook her head, knowing that couldn't be possible. Men who were only into casual relationships didn't get jealous. "Chase—" she cleared her throat to say "—I'd like you to meet my brother, Rico Claiborne."

Chase lifted a brow and stared first at her and then at the man. "Your brother?" he asked, clearly astonished. The two looked nothing alike.

"Yes, her brother," the man answered smiling. He slowly crossed the room to Chase. "And you are?" he asked as though he had every right to know. Chase started to tell him off but then he remembered how he and his brothers used to behave with his baby sister Delaney's dates, and decided big brother here was due the same courtesy.

"Chase Westmoreland."

Chase watched a confused expression form on the man's face before Rico turned around to look Jessica.

Jessica inhaled deeply. She knew that Rico recognized the Westmoreland name and had questions. And she would have to give him answers.

Rico turned back around and offered Chase his hand. "Nice meeting you, Chase Westmoreland."

Chase took the hand the man offered, wondering what the hell was going on. He had picked up on something between brother and sister when he'd given the man his name and that had him confused. "Nice meeting you as well," he finally said. He then cleared his throat and said, "I'm sure you want to visit with your sister so I'll be going."

Rico smiled. "You don't have to leave on my account."

Chase inhaled deeply. Yes, he did have to leave. He had to go somewhere and think about his possessive feelings. "I was about to go anyway. I have a lot of work to do."

Rico nodded.

"Chase owns that huge restaurant two doors down," Jessica was saying. "My shop assistant got sick today and he was kind enough to help me out with the lunch-hour crowd."

Rico Claiborne nodded again, looked over his shoulder at Jessica and then back at Chase and said, "Oh, I see."

Chase frowned. He had a feeling Jessica's brother was seeing too damn much. "Nice meeting you," he said, then crossed the room to the door. Before he opened it he stopped and glanced over at Jessica. "And I'll see you Saturday morning."

She smiled. "All right."

Chase then walked out the door and closed it behind him. For a long moment Jessica didn't say anything but watched as he walked past Mrs. Morrison's shop back toward his place.

"Would you like to tell me what's going on, Jess?"

Jessica turned and met her brother's inquisitive gaze. "I'm not sure I know, myself, Rico."

Later that night Jessica walked into the ballroom of a community center and glanced around. This was a fund-raiser for a mayoral candidate and like everyone else present, she had purchased a ticket to attend. However, she was only here to get answers from the man whose company would be catering the food.

Rico had been passing through on his way to Florida and had only stayed long enough for them to share a snack and talk. She had explained as much about the situation as she could, leaving out specific details involving her and Chase but she had a feeling he had read between the lines anyway.

Jessica glanced down at her watch. She had arrived during the cocktail hour, so it wouldn't be too difficult to make her way to the kitchen and talk to the cook. All she needed was a few minutes of his time.

Moments later she walked up to one of the waiters who was carrying around a tray of hors d'oeuvres. "I'd like to see Mr. Henry. Is he around?"

The man smiled then nodded in the direction of the kitchen. "He's in there."

"Thanks."

A few moments later she walked into the kitchen and glanced across the room at the man giving orders to a couple of waiters. If this was Theodore Henry then he was a lot younger than she'd thought he would be. This man appeared to be in his middle forties.

She waited until the two young waiters left before approaching him. "Mr. Henry?"

He turned and gave her a pleasant smile. "Yes? How can I help you?" he asked, extending his hand to her.

"I'm Jessica Claiborne. I've tried calling you several times but you never return my calls." Jessica watched as the smile on his face vanished and he coolly withdrew his hand from hers.

"I am an extremely busy man. Besides, I have no idea what you were asking about."

Jessica lifted a brow. "So you knew nothing about Scott Westmoreland's allegations that my grandfather gave you Westmoreland recipes when you were Schuster's cook?"

"Oh, I heard about it but I didn't have time for such claims. I was too busy coming up with those tasty dishes to worry about two old men with nothing better to do than argue over something unimportant."

Jessica exhaled a breath. Although it was killing her, she was determined to continue questioning the man with polite professionalism. Although she definitely wanted to tell him where he could shove his arrogant attitude. "And just where *did* you get the recipes, Mr. Henry?"

His frown deepened. "Not that I have to answer that, but to clear your mind about any wrongdoing on my part, those recipes have been in my family for years. I told Westmoreland that, but he refused to believe me."

Before giving her a chance to respond or to ask him anything else, he said, "Look, Miss Claiborne, I really don't have time to stand here and discuss something that happened almost eighteen years ago. Evidently it's important to you but it's not to me. Now if you'll excuse me, I have things to do."

"Hey, boss, we're about to leave," Donna said to Chase. "You plan to stay late tonight?"

Chase pushed away from his desk. "Not too late. I just have a little bit of paperwork I need to do."

Donna nodded. "Okay. I'll see you in the morning."

Once alone, Chase leaned back in his chair and glanced around. His office looked normal, nothing like it had the night before. But still that didn't stop the memories from flooding his insides with a heated rush.

He stood for a moment, stretching his legs. As he walked around the room every step he took reminded him of Jessica being here with him last night. He remembered all the times he had kissed her, brushed his lips across her skin, touched her with his fingers, and devoured her greedily with his mouth. He was getting hard just thinking about it.

Damn. He was spending way too much time lusting after Jessica. After all, that's all it was. There was no other explanation for it. That bout of jealousy earlier today had stemmed from possessiveness, nothing more. Hell, he'd had a right to feel possessive after what the two of them had shared. She had been a virgin, for heaven's sakes. He couldn't help but smile. Even she had been surprised by that.

He stretched his shoulders and looked down at his watch. It was close to eleven o'clock. He wondered what Jessica was doing. Was her brother still there?

What if he wasn't? He sighed deeply. Damn, but he wanted to see her.

He shook his head. After last night, if he were to show up now, this late, she'd think he was making a booty call. Hmm, although the thought of that sounded nice, he knew, whether he wanted to admit it or not, that he thought of Jessica as more than a convenient body he could use. There was something about her that reached him on all levels, not just the physical one. He wished he had the strength to keep her at arm's length but knew he could not. Even when she wasn't there with him he could feel her presence. Thoughts of her were always embedded deep in his head.

Knowing he had to get out of his office he grabbed his jacket off the rack. Moments later he was locking the door behind him. He tried not to glance over at Jessica's place. But he just couldn't help it.

Fighting temptation with a vengeance, he walked to his car. He was determined not to see Jessica again today. But as he pulled out of the parking lot, intent on going home, he knew that tomorrow was only a few hours away.

Nine

"**H**ey, Chase, you got somewhere to go tonight?"

Chase glanced up from looking at his cards and met Dare's stare. He and his brothers were over at Storm's place playing a friendly game of cards. At least it always started off friendly. Hopefully tonight they wouldn't have to worry about Storm's loud complaining when he started losing. With newborn twins in the house he figured his brother's boisterous foul mouth would be kept at a minimum.

"What makes you think I have someplace to go?" he asked.

Dare smiled. "Because you seem anxious about something, and you keep looking at your watch,"

Thorn chuckled and glanced over at Chase. "And that's a sure sign a woman is involved."

Chase had no intentions of telling them if there was or if there wasn't. It had been hard going all day without seeing Jessica. Twice he had started over to her place before quickly changing his mind. They would be seeing each other tomorrow when she went with him to Chattanooga and he was satisfied that was soon enough.

Chase threw down his cards. There wasn't a damn satisfying thing about it. He glanced around the table at his brothers, who were staring at him as if he'd lost his mind. "Look, I'm out of here," he said standing on his feet.

Stone lifted a dark brow. "But for once you're winning."

Chase inhaled. No, he wasn't winning. He was losing every minute he was sitting here with them when he could be with Jessica, in her arms, in her bed.

This had turned out to be a good batch of chocolate, Jessica thought as she pulled off her cooking mitt and licked her lips. She had made more than she needed, but she figured the extra would be perfect for moulding into candy for Chase's Crusaders.

Removing the hairnet from her head, she pushed a wayward strand of hair from her face and thought about her disappointing meeting with Theodore Henry last evening. The man was arrogant. And regardless of what he'd said, she believed he had gotten those recipes from somewhere.

Today had been a very busy day and she was glad Mrs. Stewart had felt well enough to return. But the steady stream of customers hadn't stopped her from glancing over at the door every once in a while hoping to see Chase walk in. She knew Fridays were one of the busiest days at his restaurant, but still, she had missed seeing him all day. He'd had dinner delivered to her and the thought of him thinking of her made her smile. She had discovered that Chase Westmoreland—the man she had fallen in love with—was a very thoughtful man.

She glanced around when the doorbell rang. It was close to ten o'clock. Who could that be? Her pulse rate increased at the thought that it might be Chase. Leaving the shop's kitchen, she quickly made her way to the front door. The silhouette of his body through the glass gave him away. She hadn't been expecting him but she could tell by the way her heart was beating and the sizzling heat that was beginning to flow through her that she was glad to see him.

Breathing deeply she slowly unlocked the door.

Chase couldn't help but stare at the woman standing in front of him. She was barefoot and her thick black hair was pulled back into a ponytail, but a lock of hair had escaped and obscured one eye in a way he thought was sexy.

"Chase?"

He stuffed his hands in his pockets to keep them from reaching out and pulling the rubber band from her hair, totally destroying her ponytail and making her hair tumble over her shoulders.

"I was playing cards with my brothers," he said slowly, getting turned on just by looking at her standing there. "I was winning, but I couldn't keep my mind on the game for thinking about you, wondering what you were doing and wishing whatever it was, I could be here with you." He watched Jessica's mouth turn up into a smile and his guts clenched.

"Chocolate," she said softly.

He blinked then lifted a brow. "Excuse me?"

She smiled again. "I was making chocolate. At least I was just finishing up. Would you like to come in?"

Chase smiled. Would he ever. "Are you sure you don't mind?"

She met his gaze. "I'm positive." As he closed the door behind him, Chase leaned against it for support and stared at her. Her reaction to his heated gaze seemed natural, and the darkness of his eyes touched her everywhere, making a low burning need ignite through her. Seconds turned into minutes and neither said anything. If she didn't speak soon, she'd be burned to a crisp. "Would you like some?"

Too late she realized what she'd asked and watched a smile tilt the corners of his lips. It was a smile that was definitely provocative, irrevocably male. She quickly decided to clarify. "Chocolate. I made extra. Would you like to taste some?"

He nodded his head, kept his gaze directed on her. "I'd love to taste your chocolate."

She swallowed as a sharp physical reaction sliced through her and it made her wonder if they were still discussing the same thing. "There's some left on the stove."

Chase followed Jessica to the kitchen and remembered the last time he'd been inside that particular part of the shop. It had been the night he had taken her to the movies and she had invited him in for cookies and milk afterward.

"Where's your brother?" Chase decided to ask, wondering if the two of them were alone. He hadn't seen another car parked out front."

"He's gone. He was passing through and only stayed for a little while."

Chase nodded. "I would never have guessed the two of you were related."

Jessica glanced back over her shoulder at him and smiled. Most people didn't and she understood why. "Our father is African-American but Jennifer, my stepmother, is white. Rico looks like her and my sister Savannah looks like a combination of both of them."

Chase stood just inside the door of the kitchen and glanced around as the aroma of chocolate teased his nostrils. She had definitely been busy. A long table was lined with molds for chocolate lollipops. But what was really holding his attention was Jessica.

He watched as she walked over to an industrial-sized stove. "One thing about chocolate," she was saying, "is that you can never make too much, since it can be stored and reused many times over."

She turned and smiled at him. "The only problem is that tonight I've run out of storage space and I have to get rid of what's left in the pot since I won't be using it. I think it was a really good batch." Chase watched as she stuck her hand into the pot and then tasted the chocolate from her finger.

His gut clenched at the sight of her licking her finger clean, and he felt an immediate hardening of his body as his control began slipping. He met her gaze and doubted that she knew just how aroused he was getting from watching her.

"May I have a taste?" he asked, shrugging out of his leather jacket and walking toward her. He paused long enough to place the jacket on a hook near a small table.

"Sure. Is a spoonful okay or do you want—"

"Your finger."

She lifted an arched brow. "My finger?"

He came to stand in front of her. She smelled good, but he knew without a doubt that she tasted even better. "I want to lick it off your finger. Just like you did."

Jessica swallowed hard. His words made her feel tingly all over, especially in one particular spot. She turned back to the stove and stuck her finger in the huge pot. She shivered slightly as she ran her fingertip along the side and coated it with warm chocolate. She turned and held her hand up to Chase, close to his lips. "Here you go."

Without saying anything, and without his gaze leaving hers, he caught her hand in his to steady it, then stuck out his tongue and licked the chocolate off her finger. His strokes ignited the already simmering flames inside her to a torturous blaze as she watched his tongue gently but boldly caress her finger. She felt a whimper form in her throat and when he sucked her finger into his mouth, devouring it greedily, she nearly came undone. He had to reach out and catch her by the waist to stop her from melting to a heap on the floor.

When he finally released her finger, he smiled at her, licked his lips and said, "You're right. That's a good batch. I've never had chocolate that tasted that good before." Then before she could catch her next breath, he leaned in close to her lips and whispered, "And I want some more."

He kissed her, slanting his mouth greedily over hers. His seductive attack on her mouth put her on hot alert. Immediately her body responded to the feel of her breasts pressed tightly against his chest, the way her middle fit snugly against the hard length of him, and the way his mouth was mating with hers. She could feel the desire between them intensifying. They needed each other badly. He tasted like chocolate, but she figured so did she. And they both intended to indulge to their hearts' content.

Chase finally pulled back. Breathless. Something inside him snapped. The deep sexual need for her that he'd been fighting all day swiftly uncoiled. He wanted her. Desperately. Now.

He lifted up his T-shirt. Tossing it aside, he went to the snap on his jeans. The same fever consuming him was consuming her too and he watched her undo the top two buttons of her smock and pull the cotton material over her head. Within seconds he stood before her without a stitch of clothing on and she wore only a blue bra and matching lacy thong.

Driven by a need that was unlike anything he'd ever experienced before he reached out and pulled the rubber band holding her ponytail in place, letting her hair flow wildly around her shoulders. Then, with a flick of his wrist, he unfastened her bra and slipped it off her. His gaze then went to her thong, and he reached out and traced his finger along the thin scrap of material before bending to gently pull it down her legs.

He smiled and, before Jessica was aware of what he was about to do, he reached his hand into the pot of chocolate, coated his fingers and proceeded to smear the warm, creamy richness all over her chest. She made a purring sound deep in her throat at the feel of his hands coating the dark, sticky sweet substance all over her breasts. Using his fingers and gentle precision he smoothed it all over her skin, rubbing his thumb over the sensitive peaks of her breasts before moving lower.

His hand made a path down her stomach then slid lower, spreading chocolate everywhere he touched. Jessica squeezed her eyes shut as heat suffused her body, causing a burning sensation between her legs. And when he touched her there, covering her in warm chocolate, she leaned forward and pressed her lips against his neck and whispered his name.

She opened her eyes when she felt him sweep her up into his arms and walk across the room to an unused table and placed her on it. Then his mouth was everywhere as he leaned over her and began licking the chocolate from her body. With every stroke, every caress of his tongue she moaned his name, groaned a need, and her hips involuntarily came off the table as he robbed her senses blind in the most primitive way known to mankind.

The quaking of her body alerted him that she was close to coming apart. He quickly gathered her into his arms, sat down in a chair and placed her on his lap, straddling him. Purposefully, he guided himself into her. Instinctively, as if she needed this, wanted him, she pushed her body down on the hard, pulsing erection and threw her head back as her muscles drew him in deeper, clenched him, stealing his breath with every inch of him that her body absorbed.

He pulled her mouth down to his in a kiss that was downright salacious, and he began thrusting his body upward, plunging back and forth, in and out of her, setting a rhythm that was meant to drive her.

"Chase!"

He gritted his teeth, took one final plunge and gripped her hips, locking her body to his, needing the feel of his throbbing flesh exploding within the crevices of her womanly core. The thought of what was happening, the profound degree of intimacy they were sharing, made him nudge her legs wider, wanting to give her everything he had and then some.

He heard her cry out again and then he lost it. When she began convulsing in his arms he was powerless to deny himself another orgasm. A shiver of animalistic need raced up his spine and with a growl of deep satisfaction he plunged into her again. He arched his back and called her name as the most incredible climax took control of his body and mind, sending them swirling with sensations he'd never felt before. Three nights ago he'd thought this innocent whiff of a woman was almost too much for him. Now he wondered how he would survive the passion she stirred each and every time they made love.

What he had just experienced left him weak, sensuously spent and for long moments neither of them spoke. Nor did it seem were they in a hurry to separate their bodies. They needed to remain connected a while longer.

Then he lifted his head and their gazes met and at that moment he knew that what they had shared had been earth-shatteringly special, and that no matter how many times they made love, he would never get enough of her.

And he also realized something else. Jessica Claiborne was getting under his skin, and getting deeper and deeper with every passing second.

Chase awoke to the sound of horns blasting in the distance. It was morning. He glanced over at the woman cuddled beside him, remembering all that had transpired between them the night before. After making love to her in the chair he had swept her into his arms and brought her upstairs to the shower where he washed any lingering traces of chocolate from her body. He had dried her off before sweeping her into his arms to carry her over to the bed where they made love over and over again.

He closed his eyes, thinking there was no other place he'd rather be at the moment than lying beside her. But then the thought of being deeply embedded within the warmth of her body was a damn good idea, too. An even better one. He rubbed a hand over his face. If he kept at this pace he would have to start taking an extra vitamin each day.

He glanced over at the clock. It was nearly seven. His restaurant had opened without him and since his car was parked outside and he was nowhere to be found, Donna and Kevin would be able to guess where he was and what he'd been doing.

He rubbed a hand across his chin. He needed a shave. But then a slow burn began seeping up his spine making him aware of something else that he needed.

Jessica.

Oh, hell, he had to wake her up sometime. He smiled, knowing just the way he wanted to do it.

Jessica glanced over at Chase when they passed a sign that said they had reached Chattanooga. Situated along the Tennessee River and tucked away among the southern Appalachian Mountains, it was clearly a beautiful city.

She had enjoyed Chase's company during the two-hour drive from Atlanta, although she had slept the first half hour on the road. She was still filled with memories of how he had awakened her that morning. A smile curved her lips.

She sighed as she thought about the conversation they had shared during the past hour or so. He had told her more about his and his brothers' escapades growing up, and she had shared with him memories of her times with Rico and Savannah.

After taking care of the business he had come to Chattanooga for, Chase suggested that they have lunch at a restaurant on the Formal Gardens at the Chattanooga Choo Choo. After a delicious lunch of mouth-watering seafood, they had walked around holding hands, basking in the beauty of the gardens. She hadn't known so many kinds of roses existed.

As they continued walking, enjoying the beauty of so many flowering plants, he pulled her closer to him and whispered. "Last night was special, Jessica. This entire week has been. I want you to know that."

She glanced up at him and smiled. He had told her that twice already. "Spending time with you has been special to me as well, Chase."

They were silent for a moment while they continued walking, headed toward the parking lot and back to his car. He then said, "I'd like to prepare dinner for you tomorrow."

She chuckled, remembering what happened the last time she'd shared dinner with him. "At the restaurant?"

"No, my home."

They had reached his car and stopped walking. She gazed up at him. He was smiling that smile that made her feel warm and tingly on the inside. She had gotten a quick tour of his home when they had gone there that morning for him to change clothes. She thought his home in Buckhead, a very upscale and affluent section of Atlanta, was simply beautiful.

"I've love to have dinner with you tomorrow, Chase. Do you need me to bring anything?"

A sexy smile touched his lips. "Only yourself."

She laughed quietly. "Umm, I think that can be arranged."

He pulled her into his arms and just before he kissed her, he whispered, "I most certainly hope so."

Although Chase had told her to only bring herself, Jessica couldn't resist making a delicious dessert. She smiled as she glanced down at the baking dish filled with banana pudding.

But her smile faltered, the banana pudding suddenly forgotten when Chase opened the door and her gaze connected with his. He stood before her, imposing, undeniably male and irresistibly sexy. The royal blue pullover sweater he wore emphasized very broad shoulders and his jeans fit well-built hips and firm muscular thighs perfectly. She clung tightly to the little composure that she had left while drowning in everything sensual about him.

"I thought I told you that the only thing you had to bring was yourself."

She swallowed. Good grief. His voice sounded just as sexy as the rest of him. "I couldn't resist."

He smiled, moved forward and took the dish from her hand. "And neither can I, Jessica." He leaned down and kissed her, giving any neighbors who might be out and about something to talk about.

He pulled back slightly and whispered close to her lips. "Maybe we ought to finish this inside."

She licked her lips. "Umm, yes, maybe we ought to."

He stepped back, and, as soon as she was inside with the door closed, he placed the baking dish on a hall table and pulled her into his arms, kissing her more ardently than he had a few moments ago. "Kissing you has become addictive," he whispered, as he used his tongue to lick the sides of her mouth and a section of skin beneath her earlobe. "I definitely like the way you taste."

She smiled up at him. "And here I came prepared to be fed, not to become a meal."

He chuckled against her lips before licking them some more. "Oh, don't worry, baby, I'm going to feed you." He pulled in a deep breath and took a step back. "Come on to the kitchen before I have you pinned up against that door and take you right here and now. I'm just that tempted."

He picked up the banana pudding, then bent his head down to her for another quick kiss. "I hope you have plenty of energy because I intend to put you to work."

She smiled. "Work?"

"Yes, work," he said as he led her into the kitchen. "I intend for you to help me prepare one of the Westmoreland secret family recipes for dinner tonight."

Jessica suddenly went still. "But I thought you said you didn't share the secret recipes with anyone."

He turned around, looked over at her and grinned. "It's okay—I trust you. Now come on. I told you, I planned on putting you to work."

Jessica hesitated. Now was the perfect time to level with him. She should tell him the truth, especially since her investigation had hit a brick wall. There was no one else to talk to for more information. Paula Meyers and Darcy Evans said they had told her all they knew, while Schuster and Theodore Henry claimed they knew nothing. Although there was something about Darcy Evans' and Theodore Henry's version of things that she didn't believe, she had no proof to base her suspicions on. But she wasn't ready to throw in the towel. She was determined to speak to both of them again.

"Jessica?"

She glanced over at Chase. He was looking at her strangely. "Yes?"

"Are you okay?"

She inhaled deeply, wanting to tell him the truth. But she knew at this moment she couldn't. She couldn't risk what he might do. What if he kicked her out on her butt. She couldn't stand that right now. She would tell him the truth soon. But not today.

She forced a smile. "I'm okay. What do you want me to do?"

Chase placed a typed piece of paper on the counter in front of her. "I've got the recipe memorized but since you're helping I printed it off the computer."

She breathed in as she glanced down at the recipe. "You keep secret recipes stored in your computer?"

He chuckled as he pulled a can of cream out of the refrigerator. "Yes, I intend to pass my business on to one of my nieces or nephews one day."

"What about kids of your own?"

He glanced over at her. The smile he wore wavered just a tad. "I have no intentions of getting married and I don't plan on ever having any. And on the off chance that I do marry—probably a good twenty or thirty years from now—all I'd want from my wife is companionship. Our marriage will be in name only."

Jessica nodded and glanced back down at the piece of paper. Even the thought of a fifty-something Chase marrying a woman in a marriage of convenience bothered her. She loved him, dammit!

"So what do you think?"

His question almost started her. She'd been so wrapped up in her thoughts. "About what? You getting married twenty years from now to a woman you won't love?"

He shook his head and smiled wryly. "No. What do you think about the recipe? Are you up to it?"

He placed the cream on the counter and came to stand directly behind her. He reached out and drew her back against him, her tush snug against his erection. If anyone was up to anything, he most certainly was. She sucked in a quick breath when he slid his hands down past her waist to her hips.

She slowly closed her eyes. At any moment he would start inching up her skirt to slide his hand underneath. From there he would find his way into her panties. If she didn't stop him they would never get dinner done. Besides, she needed a few moments alone to pull herself together. Their conversation about the possibility of him getting married one day had messed with her mind.

She spun around quickly, almost startling him in the process. "Excuse me. I need to wash up before we get started."

Without giving him a chance to say anything, she eased by him, went into the hall bathroom, closed the door and tried to catch her breath..

After finishing off the last piece of baked chicken on her plate, Jessica leaned back in her chair and licked her lips. Every meal that Chase had prepared for her had made her want seconds. But what was so special about the baked chicken and Westmoreland rice was that they had prepared the meal together—working side by side in his kitchen as though they belonged there.

"Don't lick your lips like that," Chase murmured from across the table.

She glanced over at him and raised her eyebrows. "Why not?"

"Because it makes me want to lean over this table and lick them for you."

The air between them started to simmer, and Chase felt the need to take a step back, slow things down, savor their evening together. "Tell me about your grandparents."

She quickly glanced over at him. Panic suddenly fill her. "Why?"

"Because I think considering what you told me about your mother's situation that your grandparents must have had a positive effect on your life."

She smiled. His expression warmed her, and she could tell that he was truly interested. Memories of her grandparents flashed through her mind. "They did. Although my mom and I had our own place, my grandparents were close by." She paused before adding. "They moved to California to be near me and my mom when I was around ten or so. My greatest memories are the ones I shared with them."

Jessica knew that now would be the perfect time to tell Chase that she was Carlton Graham's granddaughter and suddenly decided to do so. "Chase."

He met her gaze and smiled. "Yes?"

She made a small sound in her throat but couldn't get the words out. At least not those words. Instead, she cleared her throat and asked. "How long have you lived here?"

"A little more than a year. Before then I had an apartment in Roswell. I visited a friend in this area and decided I liked it. What about you? Do you plan to live over your shop for a while or are you interested in buying a house someplace?"

Jessica took a sip of her coffee. "I owned a home in Sacramento. It was larger than I needed, but my boss at the corporation where I used to work believed that a big house in a posh neighborhood was a must for the attorneys he employed. And, like an obedient soldier, I did what was expected."

He nodded. "Do you miss being a lawyer?"

She shrugged. "I miss practicing law but not the corporate politics that went along with it. The straw that broke the camel's back was a case I was assigned to work on. One of the divisions of a company I represented made children's toys. We had repeatedly gotten complaints that one particular toy was dangerous and several kids had gotten injured playing with it. But it was a big moneymaker and the company refused to pull it from the shelves. When a child died, we got sued. I had to defend a product that I knew had been responsible for causing that child's death. I couldn't do it and quit."

Chase felt a rush of admiration for her. Instead of getting caught up in the woes of corporate politics and becoming just another company robot, she had taken a stand and had made what had to have been tough decisions regarding her future.

He stood, walked around the table and took her hand in his. "Come on, let's go for a walk."

She lifted a surprised brow. "A walk?"

He smiled. "Yes, the neighborhood has a nature trail. And usually around this time of the evening you can catch a fox or two roaming around. Besides, walking is a good way to work off that huge meal we just ate. And just think we haven't gotten into the banana pudding yet."

She grimaced. "Hey, don't remind me. I don't know where I'll be able to put anything else."

He grinned. "That's what you get for having a hard head. I told you not to bring anything but yourself."

A smile touched her lips. "Well, yeah, but I didn't want

you to do all the cooking. Had I known you would put me to work I would have thought twice about doing it."

He leaned over and pressed a kiss to her temple. "You enjoyed sharing the kitchen with me today. Admit it."

Jessica laughed. "Okay, I admit it. Are you happy?"

He raised his hand and cupped her face in it. He smiled down at her and held her gaze. "Yes, I am happy," he said quietly, actually meaning it. His hand tightened around hers. "Come on, let's get out of here and take that walk."

"What do you mean you haven't told him yet?"

Later that night Jessica stared down into the cup of coffee she held in her hand. She had her sister on speaker phone and Savannah hadn't wasted any time giving her the third degree.

"Jessica?"

She raised her eyes to the ceiling. This was worse than Savannah being here in person. Her tone was just that effective. "I hear you," Jessica said, taking a sip of coffee. Moments later she added. "The timing has never been right. Every time I get ready to open my mouth, he says something sweet and I can't bring myself to tell him."

"Sounds like you're making excuses."

Jessica sighed deeply. She was. "It's not easy, Savannah. I told you how I feel about him."

"Yes, but in order to give him a chance to feel that same way about you, you have to be honest with him. Put all your cards on the table."

Jessica gazed down into her cup of coffee again. Of course her sister was right. While having dinner with Chase that evening she had had at least two opportunities to come clean and tell him the truth, but had taken advantage of neither. "If I told him now, without proof of my grandfather's innocence he might think the worst."

"And what if you can't prove your granddad was innocent, Jess? What then?"

Jessica didn't want to think about that possibility. Both Darcy Evans and Theodore Henry were hiding something. She could feel it. She closed her eyes and saw the image of a very handsome Chase Westmoreland smiling at her. Then suddenly another image invaded. It was one of Chase angry at her. The sexy line of his mouth had transformed into a deep frown.

"Jess?"

Jessica opened her eyes again. "Yes?"

"You're special, and no matter what the outcome might be, if he doesn't see how special you are then you're better off without him."

"You think too highly of me, sis," Jessica laughed as she pushed her coffee cup aside. She'd had enough caffeine for one day.

"Hey, I can say the same about you."

For a long moment, neither said anything and then Jessica broke the silence. "You would like him," she said quietly.

"Yes, but as far as I'm concerned, he's already taken. You did say he has brothers didn't you?"

Jessica grinned. "They're taken as well, however he has some very good-looking single cousins."

"Umm, maybe I should come for a visit."

"You know," Jessica said smiling. "Maybe you should."

* * *

"Storm says you're pretty serious about some woman."

Chase glanced over at his cousin Quade who had made an unexpected visit to town. Quade worked behind the scenes for the Secret Service and his job protecting the president could take him anywhere. Chase took a sip of his beer before saying. "Storm talks too damn much."

Quade smiled. "Maybe he does." He thought a moment, then said, "So tell me…who is she and how did she manage to get under your skin?"

Chase shrugged one shoulder. Although he rarely saw Quade these days, that didn't diminish their friendship, best buddies since childhood, who rarely kept secrets from each other. "Her name is Jessica Claiborne and she moved here from California. She used to be a corporate attorney but got fed up with corporate politics and decided to try her hand at baking instead. She owns a confectionary two doors down from the restaurant."

Quade lifted a brow. "She gave up law to make candy?"

Chase sat back and smiled. "Yes."

Quade shook his head. "That was some career move. I wondered what her parents thought of that."

Chase spent the next ten minutes or so telling Quade about Jessica's past and her bastard of a father. "That had to have been hard on her," Quade said.

Chase nodded. "I'm sure it was, but, at least she had her grandparents."

Quade sighed. "Yes. It sounds like they were good people."

Chase thought of the woman who was beginning to mean a lot to him. "I'm glad they were there for her."

Quade sat forward. "So how did she managed to capture your attention?"

Chase stood and walked to the window. He remain silent for a moment pondering Quade's question. He turned from the window and shrugged broad shoulders. "Hell, that's a good question, but she's there, Quade, under my skin and the strange thing about it is that I sort of like her there."

Chase saw the surprised smile that touched his cousin's lips. "Next time I'm passing through I'd like to meet her."

"You will," Chase promised.

Ten

"What are you thinking about, Jessica?"

Jessica glanced up and met Chase's gaze. She had been staring down at their clasped hands as they sat at a coffee shop in Lenox Square Mall, thinking how comforting it felt for her fingers to be intertwined in his.

A week and a half had passed since she'd had dinner with him at his home and each and every day she spent with him she was falling deeper and deeper in love. But hanging over her head was the fact that she wasn't being completely honest with him.

Theodore Henry had gotten downright rude and even threatened to file harassment charges if she tried contacting him again. That meant her only hope was Darcy Evans, who hadn't returned any of her calls. She would make it her business to talk to the woman again.

She knew Chase was waiting for an answer, so she forced a smile and said, "Umm, I was just thinking about what a close-knit family you have." And she really meant that. Chase had invited her to a Monday-night football party at Jared and Dana's home to see the Falcons play the Cowboys. They had watched the game on Jared's state-of-the-art home-theater system. She had met Chase's parents and reacquainted herself with some of the family members she had met previously. And she had finally met his sister Delaney and her husband Sheikh Jamal Ari Yasir.

He smiled. "Yes, I have to admit that we are that. I can't imagine it being any other way." He leaned closer to her. "But you and your siblings are close, too, aren't you?"

She nodded. "Yes. Savannah and Rico are great. Jennifer has a sister and a brother but they're standoffish. They think she went a little too far including me in her family. After all, I'm the product of her husband's affair."

"You were also her husband's child. Besides, her husband's wrongdoing wasn't your fault. I think it was admirable of her to accept that and do what she did. But I know that many women's pride would not have let them do it."

Jessica nodded again. "Yes, I know, and that's what makes her so special to me. She made it her business to include me as part of Savannah's and Rico's life and I appreciate her for it. It really helped after Mom's died."

"I'm sure it was hard on your grandparents to lose your mother that way."

Jessica sighed deeply. "Yes, she was their only child. For a while my grandfather blamed himself for not finding out about my father sooner. Another part of him questioned whether he had done the right thing at all by hiring that investigator and telling my mother the truth. He never thought she would take her life over it."

Jessica didn't say anything for a while, then added, "For the longest time I was bitter and resented her for what she did, leaving me alone. I had to go through grief counseling to let go finally and realize that the love my mother had for my father was an obsession and a sickness. That's when I promised myself that I would never get that caught up over a man."

Chase tightened his fingers around Jessica's as he once again thought about the relationship they shared. He had to admit that the past couple of weeks had been pretty darn special. They had attended a laser show on Stone Mountain, played tennis together twice and she had watched Chase's Crusaders clinch another win one week only to lose big-time the next. Last Sunday evening, a pack of them led by Thorn had taken their Thorn-Byrd motorcycles on the road to ride all the way to Augusta for dinner. No one in the family had seemed surprised that he'd brought Jessica along, nor had anyone questioned him about the amount of time the two of them were spending together. His family had accepted that they were now an item. He wasn't sure how he felt about that.

"More coffee?"

They both glanced up at the waiter who was making his rounds. "No thanks," Chase replied, releasing Jessica's hand to glance at his watch. "In fact, I'd appreciate our bill now."

When the waiter left, Chase smiled over at Jessica. "Thanks for going shopping with me."

She chuckled. "There aren't many people I know, men specifically, who do early Christmas shopping. You still have two months left."

Chase grinned. "Yes, but like you said, I have a large family. Besides, giving out gift cards makes it easy. The kicker is trying to decide what stores they like best." His grin widened. "The saying 'beggars can't be choosers' doesn't always apply in my family."

After finishing their coffee they walked around the mall again. Although there were two months lefts before Christmas, many of the stores already had their holiday decorations up.

"This place is like a madhouse the day after Thanksgiving. You'll have to come with me that Friday to see what I mean. But the crowd puts me in the Christmas spirit."

Jessica suddenly felt breathless. Thanksgiving was a month away. That he assumed they would still be together had her walking on air. But she quickly came back down to earth when she thought of what was still lurking over her head. She decided to pay Darcy Evans another visit tomorrow. She had to give it one more try before finally telling Chase the truth.

Jessica was grateful Mrs. Stewart had agreed to work a full day so that she could make the trip to Macon to pay Darcy Evans another visit. She hated being a nuisance, but she was determined to give it another try to see if perhaps there was something the woman wasn't telling her.

Darcy wasn't at home but an older woman—Darcy's

mother—told her that Darcy owned a hair salon not far away. Thirty minutes later Jessica was parking in front of Darcy's Beauty Box.

Jessica knew the moment she walked into the shop and her gaze connected with Darcy that the woman was surprised to see her. "Ms. Evans, how are you?" she asked, extending her hand. The set-up of the shop was very chic. Jessica was glad there was only one customer sitting under the hair dryer, who wouldn't be able to overhear their conversation.

"Why are you here?" Darcy asked, reluctantly accepting the hand Jessica offered. "I thought we finished our discussion the last time we talked."

A wry smile touched Jessica's lips. "I was hoping that perhaps you might have remembered something else since then."

"No, there's nothing else. I told you everything I know."

"Are you sure?"

Darcy tore her gaze from Jessica's and glanced around the room, looking anywhere other than Jessica's eyes. "Yes, I'm sure."

Jessica still wasn't completely certain and decided to try another angle. She didn't want to push but she needed the truth. "Do you believe my grandfather passed those recipes on to someone who worked at Schuster's, Mrs. Evans?"

Darcy's eyes snapped back to hers. "No, of course not. He was one of the most honest men that I knew. I felt bad when Mr. Westmoreland accused him of doing that."

Jessica lifted a brow. "You were there the day it happened?"

"No. Your grandfather and Mr. Westmoreland had an argument and then your grandfather quit. But he and Mr. Westmoreland were such good friends we all assumed he would be coming back."

Jessica nodded. "Do you remember what the argument was about?"

She watched as the woman tore her gaze away from her again. A few moments passed then she said quietly, "It was about me."

Jessica wasn't sure she'd heard her correctly. "About you?"

The woman nodded. "I was going through a difficult time. My son Jamie who was only eighteen months old at the time was constantly sick, which kept me from work a lot. And when I was there I was so preoccupied worrying about him I was beginning to get my orders messed up."

Darcy inhaled deeply as if remember that time. "Some of the customers started complaining to Mr. Westmoreland. Your grandfather knew how much I needed my job to pay for Jamie's medical bills and asked Mr. Westmoreland to give me another chance. They argued about it. Then I heard your grandfather walked out."

The woman shook her head regretfully. "I felt bad about everything. But Paula Meyers, who had worked with your grandfather and Mr. Westmoreland a lot longer, told me not to worry about it because your grandfather had quit before after having words with Mr. Westmoreland and would be back. When two weeks went by and he didn't return, I got worried and started blaming myself."

Jessica's eyes began softening. All it took was a close look at Darcy Evans to know she was still blaming herself. "I think my grandfather and Mr. Westmoreland would have eventually patched up things, too," she decided to say. "But a couple of things happened right after that. My mother had to be hospitalized for pneumonia and my grandparents flew to California to take care of me."

Jessica smiled, remembering. "While they were there I think they decided that my mom and I needed them closer, especially when they couldn't talk her into moving to Atlanta. They returned home a week or so later and my grandfather found out about Mr. Westmoreland's accusations. His integrity had been questioned by someone he considered a good friend and he was hurt. Nothing he said to Mr. Westmoreland could prove his innocence, and I think that was one of the reasons he felt moving to California was best for everyone."

For a long moment neither she nor Darcy said anything. But Jessica could swear the older woman had an odd look on her face. And if she wasn't mistaken, it was a guilty one. "Are you sure there isn't anything else you can tell me, Ms. Evans?"

For a brief moment Darcy didn't answer, and then she said, "No, there's nothing else."

Jessica still didn't believe her. "It's important to me that if you do remember anything you contact me. I'm caught in the middle of a bad situation right now."

Darcy lifted a brow. "What kind of a bad situation?"

Jessica knew she had to be completely honest with Darcy and hoped the woman would eventually tell her whatever she was holding back. "I've fallen in love with Scott Westmoreland's grandson Chase."

Darcy nodded. "He's the one that owns that restaurant in downtown Atlanta, right?"

Jessica smiled. "Yes, that's right."

"I always knew he would be the one who would eventually follow in his grandfather's footsteps. He would hang around the restaurant and help out more than any of the others. He always seemed like a nice young man."

Jessica smile widened. "He is. We've been seeing each other for about three weeks now, but he doesn't have any idea that I'm Carlton Graham's granddaughter."

Darcy raised a surprised brow. "He doesn't?"

"No. Because of what happened all those years ago, bad blood was left between the two families. I promised my grandmother before she died that I'd prove my grandfather's innocence to the Westmorelands and end the feud." She inhaled deeply. "I hadn't planned on meeting and falling in love with Chase."

Darcy nodded. "But surely something that happened years ago wouldn't keep the two of you apart."

Jessica smiled wryly. "It might. He was pretty close to his grandfather and I can tell he's still pretty bitter about the entire thing. Besides, honesty means a lot to Chase. I should have told him who I was from the beginning. But I wanted to prove my grandfather's innocence before doing that. Now I can see I made a mistake in waiting."

"What will you do now?"

"Tell him the truth and hope he believes me. Hope he's willing to put the past behind us and move on."

Darcy didn't say anything for a few moments, then asked, "Do you think he will?"

"God, I hope so."

Chase glanced down at his watch thinking Jessica should have returned by now. He had stopped by the shop at closing time to let her know that he had to leave town unexpectedly, and found Mrs. Stewart was still there. The only thing she would tell him was that Jessica had an errand to run and she didn't expect her back before seven o'clock that night.

He couldn't help wondering what sort of errand Jessica had to do that could have kept her away from the shop practically all day. He glanced around when he heard a knock at his office door. "Who is it?"

"Donna."

"Come in."

He watched his most dependable waitress walk nervously into the room. In the months she had worked for him he'd never known Donna to be nervous about anything. But a part of him saw beyond that. For a split second he could see a hint of sadness behind those big brown eyes of hers.

When she didn't say anything he decided to urge her on. "Donna, what can I do for you?"

She looked away, hesitated, then she said, "I came to give you this."

Chase's eyesbrows shot up when she handed him a piece of paper she had in her hand. It took him a quick second to scan it. His eyes widened, and he lifted his gaze, giving her a surprised look. "You're quitting?"

She looked away again and shrugged her shoulders. "Yes. I like working here but I need to start going to school full-time if I ever want to finish. I got a letter yesterday from a college in Tennessee offering me a scholarship to finish my last two years, and I've decided to take it."

Chase smiled. Although he regretted losing Donna, he knew that was an offer that was too good to pass up. Opportunities like that didn't come often. "I'm happy for you, Donna."

At last a smile touched her lips. "Thanks. I'm pretty happy for myself. I keep rereading the letter to make sure I'm not dreaming. They want me to start in January, which means I'll have to pack up and move. With the holidays coming up I didn't want to leave you in a fix, and I wanted to let you know now, although I can probably work another month."

"And I appreciate that. You're going to be hard to replace. And if you ever need anything I'll always be a phone call away."

"Thanks, Chase."

After Donna left, Chase leaned back in his chair. He glanced down at his watch again. He had taken just about all he could stand. He needed to see Jessica. And the thought that he would be leaving town for three days didn't help matters. Hell. He'd been pretty useless all day for thinking about her. To go to her shop and not find her there had been a huge disappointment.

Chase didn't like the way his thoughts were going—he was becoming more and more obsessed with Jessica. For the first time in his life, while holding Storm's twins earlier that day when Jayla had stopped by to meet Storm for lunch, he had actually thought of having kids of his own. For Pete's sake! Just the other day he had told Jessica he didn't plan on ever having kids. Yet when he had looked down at his nieces, he'd actually envisioned Jessica as his children's mother. Panic rose thick in his throat.

He stood, suddenly not feeling at all like himself. He was encountering emotions that were best left alone. Yet for some reason he couldn't leave them alone. Not today. A sharp rush of desire flooded his insides and his main thought as he walked out of his office was that he had to see Jessica.

Chase practically launched himself at Jessica, pulling her into his arms and kissing her the moment she opened the door.

"God, I missed you today," he murmured, easing her back into the shop and closing the door shut with the heel of his shoe. He didn't care that he'd just seen her yesterday and had made love to her last night. That was then and this was now. He leaned down and kissed her.

Jessica tried not to shiver from all the love she felt flowing through every part of her body. She didn't want to think about the possibility that once she told Chase the truth tonight, he would walk away angry and not look back. But she knew what she had to do.

She pulled her mouth from his. "Chase, I have something to tell—"

Before she could finished what she was about to say, he was kissing her again, deeply, with an urgency that obliterated all her thoughts. Knowing this might very well be the last time she shared such intimacy with him, she went for sheer pleasure and attacked his mouth with the same urgency with which he was attacking hers. Moments later they were both groaning out loud.

Chase finally broke contact with her mouth, swept her into his arms and quickly carried her up the stairs. He placed her on her feet next to the bed and immediately began removing her shirt as she reached for the fly of his jeans. Both were crazed with passion, driven by need. Their level of desire had reached a boiling point.

"I want you so bad I ache," Chase whispered when he had completely removed her clothes and she had removed his. He tumbled her back on the bed, went for her breasts and greedily began licking the swollen mounds. She moaned out loud when he sucked a nipple into his mouth. His tongue began licking it, tugging on it; he was driving her crazy by holding the sensitive tip gently between his teeth and not letting go. He then gave the other breast the same torturous treatment.

"Chase!"

"Hold on, baby, I've just gotten started," he murmured, leaving her breasts to travel downward. Jessica sucked in air when his tongue began licking around her navel, circling it, branding it, kissing it.

Then he lifted his head, locked his gaze with hers and something flickered in his eyes; the heat of it made her breath catch just seconds before he lowered his mouth to her feminine core. Her legs automatically spread for him and it took all the strength that she possessed not to come off the bed under the onslaught of his skillful

mouth. But nothing could stop her from shivering un-
controllably when he increased the pressure of his
tongue, stroking her with a decadent lick that sent blood
throbbing through her veins. She screamed his name but
that only spurred him on, making him even more intent
on savoring her this way. And when an orgasm hit, splin-
tering her body into a million pieces, she screamed his
name again and bucked her hips upward as he continued to ply her with quick and sure strokes of his tongue.

It was only when the last shiver had touched her
body that he finally dragged his mouth away. Every
inch of her felt sensitive from such a fiery response. He
sat back on his haunches and the smile that played at
the corners of his lips sent shivers racing through her
again. He held her gaze, making her heart pound and she
felt an agonizing ache rekindle between her legs.

As if he knew just what she was going through, he
reached out and touched her there, began caressing her
wet flesh. Then he leaned toward her and, in a voice that
was deep, sexy and husky, he said, "Don't relax now,
sweetheart. I'm just getting warmed up."

Chase intended to make love to his woman all night.
His woman.
He closed his eyes when a sharpness tore through his
heart, almost knocking the breath out of him.
"Chase, are you okay?"
He opened his eyes and gazed down at Jessica. He
moved to position his body over her, satisfied that she
was primed and ready to take him in. At that moment,
he knew. She *was* his woman and he loved her. He loved

her. He had never intended for such a thing to happen. But it had and there wasn't a damn thing he could do about it but accept it. And he did, without question.

"Chase?"

His heart pounded against his chest and he leaned down and kissed her lips softly. "Yeah, I'm okay, baby. At this moment I couldn't be better."

She smiled cheekily up at him and said, "Hey, I think that's for me to decide."

Chase grinned as he traced her lips with the tip of his tongue. "Then let me help you make such an important decision."

And then he was back at her lips with that skillful mouth of his, kissing her deeply as his tongue whirled around in her mouth, feasting, tasting, corner to corner, marking every single crevice.

Jessica moaned and closed her eyes when he slipped his hand between their bodies. His fingers touched the soft flesh between her legs, lightly stroking, making small erotic circles, causing sensations to flood her, making her hips buck again.

He finally released her mouth and gazed down at her as she slowly opened her eyes. He was filled with an urgency that he'd never felt before by the recognition of just how much he wanted this woman. Just how much he loved her. And suddenly he became caught up in a raging desire to be inside her.

Now.

He lifted her hips with his hands, anchored his thighs between hers and positioned his aroused member dead center where he needed it to be.

He eased inside her and she automatically adjusted her body to accommodate him, lifting her hips as he went deeper. He arched his hips and pressed forward until he reached the hilt and was buried deep inside her. He fought the urge to move, to stroke her with the rhythm that would send them both over the edge. He wanted to savor being this way, inside her, locked in tight, feeling the moist heat of her clutching him, nearly stealing his breath away.

But he refused to move just yet. He held her gaze, and because he wanted her to know just how he felt at that moment—submerged in the intensity of his love—he whispered, "I love you, Jessica."

He watched her eyes widen, her face fill with disbelief, and then he saw the tears that filled her eyes, the look of happiness on her lips when she said, "I love you, too, Chase."

Damn. He hadn't expected that. And her words were the catalyst that broke his control. His need to make love to her suddenly became as vital as his need to draw his next breath. He began moving inside her in rapid thrusts, stunned by how emotions had taken over his mind, invaded his heart, filled him with a drive to make her truly his.

Never had he known anything as beautiful as what he was sharing with her now. She was filling an emptiness inside of him that he hadn't known existed. And she was doing it in a way no other woman had. His body continued moving in and out of her as she lifted her hips, wrapped her legs around his waist to hold him tight, melding their bodies together over and over.

"Chase!"

When she cried out his name, he gritted his teeth as the same sensations that began wracking her body invaded his. An explosion erupted and mind-whirling sensations overtook them. He grasped her hips while he continued to ply her with fluid strokes and the full impact of his release. It seemed they were spiraling higher than they had ever gone before, riding wave after wave of sensation so intense he wondered if he could survive. He drove into her again and again as words of love flowed from his lips.

And when his body exploded a second time, and moments later a third, he knew that she was truly his just as he was undeniably hers.

Hours later, Chase tried not to wake Jessica as he eased out of bed. He needed to leave, go home and pack for his trip to Houston. His plane would be leaving in five hours and he would be battling morning traffic to the airport.

After putting on his clothes he walked back over to the bed, leaned down and gently kissed her lips. Moments later he slipped downstairs, deciding to leave her a note. He would also call her when he got to the airport. If this meeting wasn't so important he would change his mind about going. But lately he'd given thought to opening another Chase's Place in Texas and the group of men he was meeting with could make such a venture possible.

He opened the door to her office and glanced around. This was the first time he had been in this particular room and liked how she had things set up. It was small but furnished professionally. He walked over to the stylish oak desk to get a piece of paper and a pen. His hand went still when his gaze fell on a small framed photograph.

He picked it up, blinking, not sure he was seeing straight. It was a photo of Jessica with an older couple who he could only assume were the grandparents she loved. Chase recognized the older couple immediately. They were Carlton and Helen Graham.

Suddenly, he felt as if he'd been punched in the gut. Jessica was Carlton Graham's granddaughter? If that was true, then why hadn't she told him? His hand shook as he placed the picture frame back on the desk. He glanced around and a piece of paper caught his attention. He picked it up. He read the words written on her To Do list for today:

Talk to Donald Schuster again regarding the Westmoreland recipes.

The paper slipped from his hand as he felt a stabbing sensation in his heart. He closed his eyes in denial. There was no way another Graham was betraying a Westmoreland. It couldn't be possible. When he opened his eyes and stared at the paper and the photo once again, he saw that anything was possible. Had Schuster heard that he was thinking about franchising and made some kind of deal with Jessica to get close to him? Damn, she *had* gotten close to him, and he had even trusted her enough to share one of the recipes with her. What was in it for her? A chance to sell her sweets in all the Schuster restaurants around the country? He clenched his teeth. It hurt like hell to know she was an opportunist, just like Iris had been.

He felt angrier than he'd ever felt in his life, anger mingled with deeply entrenched pain. He left the office and raced back up the stairs. For the second time in his life he had given his heart to a woman and look what happened. Never again would he trust blindly.

He felt a tightening around his heart when he walked back into Jessica's bedroom. His body was torn with the love he felt for her and the hurt her betrayal was causing. Exhaling deeply, as if that could expel any emotions he felt for her, he walked over to the bed. "Jessica, wake up."

Fighting sleep, Jessica slowly opened her eyes when she heard the sound of Chase's voice. When he came into focus she saw that he was standing over her with features filled with anger. She pulled herself up in bed. "What's wrong, Chase?"

For a moment he didn't say anything; he just looked at her and the anger was there, clearly, in his eyes. "Chase, please tell me what's wrong."

"Why didn't you tell me you were Carlton Graham's granddaughter? Did you get a kick out of playing me for a fool?"

She sucked in a quick breath, wondering how he had found out, but then knowing it really didn't matter. He *had* found out and she hadn't been the one to tell him. "No, that's not it at all, Chase. I wanted to tell you but thought I could prove my grandfather's innocence first."

"You can't prove what isn't true."

Jessica was out of bed in a flash. She got into Chase's

face, not caring that she was completely naked. "My grandfather didn't take any recipes and I wanted to prove it. But then I fell in love with you and—"

"Hell, you didn't fall in love with me. It was nothing but an act. Do you think I'm stupid, Jessica? I saw that note about you meeting with Schuster today. Are the two of you working together to pry more recipes out of a Westmoreland? What did he offer you? A chance to peddle your sweets in his restaurants?"

Jessica shook her head. "No. How could you think something like that? Schuster has answers. Someone gave him those recipes all those years ago, and since I knew it wasn't my grandfather, I met with him once to see what he could tell me. I'm meeting with him again to get more information out of him if I can."

Chase drew in a deep breath. He wanted to believe her, but all he could think about was her betraying his love. His mouth tightened in a harsh line. "If any of what you're saying is true, why didn't you tell me who you were? We've been seeing each other for almost a month, Jessica, and during that time you've had every opportunity to tell me the truth, but you never mentioned you were related to Carlton."

Jessica swallowed, knowing he had her there. There had been opportunities when she could have shared that fact with him. "Like I told you, Chase, I wanted to prove his innocence first. I was going to tell you when you first got here last night, but I didn't get a chance to. You've got to believe me. Chase. I love you and—"

Chase laughed. It was an unforgiving sound. "Love?

Is this how you show your love? By being deceitful? Then I don't want any part of it."

He turned and walked out of the room. Jessica held her breath until she heard the door slam shut behind him. Tears flooded her eyes. She had made a complete mess of things. She hadn't cleared her grandfather's name, and worse—Chase hated her.

Eleven

Chase slipped out of bed. Whenever he traveled he made it a point to stay at the best hotels. But a nice room and a soft bed couldn't prevent his restless nights.

For the past two days he had been so thickly involved with business negotiations that he hadn't allowed anything or anyone to invade his thoughts…other than Jessica. She had managed to wiggle inside his head, although he hadn't wanted her there.

And he couldn't get her out no matter how hard he tried.

Without wanting them to, memories of that night came back to flood his mind. She had actually looked shocked by his accusation. Well, hell, how had she expected him to react? Had she thought he would embrace her with open arms? Overlook the fact that his grand-

father and hers had ended up bitter enemies? For
heaven's sake, she was a Graham and he was a Westmoreland. He distinctively remembered his grandfather's warning never to trust a Graham. Not only had he
trusted one, he had fallen in love with one.

He sighed deeply. And did she actually think he
would believe her story about trying to prove her grandfather innocent? That the only reason she had met with
Schuster was to find out the truth?

But then he couldn't dismiss the possibility that his
reluctance to believe her was the reason she hadn't lev-
eled with him in the beginning. She had known he
wouldn't embrace her with open arms. They would have
become enemies before having the chance to become
friends.

On top of knowing that, there was this thought that
had been nagging at him for the past two days. What if
she *was* telling the truth? He couldn't let go of the fact
that this was a woman who had walked away from a
prestigious career for ethical reasons. A woman of
strong values and beliefs. She was also a woman who
had spent her free time baking goodies for the guys on
his team. This was someone who definitely cared about
others.

And more than anything, he couldn't forget that she
had been celibate for eight years. He had a gut feeling
it would have taken more than the promise of her products being sold in a Schuster restaurant for her to go
as far with him as she'd gone if she didn't really care
for him.

He inhaled deeply. Had he acted irrationally two

days ago? Had he been unfair by jumping to conclusions and not listening to her side of things? Had he been wrong to place her in the same category as Iris? The two women were nothing alike. Iris was an unscrupulous taker. Jessica was an extraordinary giver.

He glanced over at the clock on the nightstand. It was almost midnight. He wanted to call Jessica, talk to her. When he returned to Atlanta tomorrow he would listen to what she had to say and not be so quick to judge. No matter what, he still loved her. What happened with the Westmoreland recipes no longer mattered to him. If Jessica was hell-bent on proving her grandfather's innocence then he would help her discover how the recipes got into the wrong hands.

He took a deep breath. More than anything he wanted a future with the woman he loved.

"Listen, Jessica, if he loved you two days ago then he loves you now. Nobody can turn love on and off like a faucet, not if it's the real thing."

Jessica heard her stepmother's words but she still wasn't convinced. She had seen the look of loathing in Chase's eyes just moments before he'd left. But then she couldn't erase the memory of another look as well. It had been the look he'd given her just moments before whispering that he loved her. When he had said those words she had believed in her heart that he had meant them, just like she had meant what she'd said to him. She loved him, too.

"Even after I found out what your father had done," Jennifer was saying, "I couldn't hate him. I was hurt and

I put up a wall to protect myself from further pain, but the love was still there for a long time."

"It doesn't matter," Jessica said softly. "Chase let me know things are over between us." After a brief pause she said, "I've made some decisions."

There was a short silence, then Jennifer asked, "What sort of decisions?"

Jessica took a deep breath. "I met with a real estate agent today. I've decided to sell this place and move back to California."

"And return to law?"

"Possibly, but it won't be as a corporate attorney. I'm thinking of becoming a consumer attorney specializing in product safety."

"Do you think running away will solve anything, Jessica?"

"I'm not running away. I'm protecting my heart from further damage."

There was a brief pause again, and then Jennifer said, "Well, I think you and Chase need to sit down and talk things through."

"So do I," Jessica said quietly. "But before he left I got the distinct impression that he doesn't want to see me again. And since our businesses are separated by only one building, there's no way we can avoid seeing each other. One of us will have to leave. It might as well be me." After a brief pause she added, "Hey, I'm a survivor. You know that."

She sighed deeply. She *had* let Chase become too important to her. She had done the one thing she'd always promised herself she wouldn't do, give her heart and soul to a man. That made it harder to walk away. But walk away she would.

"What do you mean she's selling her place?" Chase asked staring hard at Donna. He had come straight to the restaurant from the airport to find Delicious Cravings closed in the middle of the day with a For Sale sign in the window.

Donna leaned back against his closed office door. "Rumor has it that she's moving back to California."

A chill of fear ripped down his spine. God, he'd been a fool to think the worst about her. He had done a lot of thinking over the past three days, and in his heart he knew Jessica loved him. He had been a complete idiot to accuse her of all those things. Unlike Iris, Jessica couldn't relate to greed.

Donna cleared her throat. "I know this might not be a good time but there's someone here who insists on seeing you."

Chase lifted an eyebrow. "Who?"

"A woman named Darcy Evans."

Chase's brow lifted higher upon remembering the name. He sighed deeply. "Please show her in."

A few minutes later, Darcy Evans walked into his office. Although she had only worked with his grandfather for a short while, no more than six months, he remembered her. She had been quiet and kept to herself, much as Donna was inclined to do.

Chase crossed the room to shake her hand. "Ms.

Evans, it's been years. It's good to see you again. Please have a seat."

When she had taken the chair across from his desk he met her gaze and asked. "What can I do for you?" Chase couldn't help noticing that she appeared nervous.

"I wanted to talk to Ms. Claiborne but her place is closed up. She came to see me a couple of times during the past month."

Chase knew he looked puzzled and confused. "Jessica came to see you?"

"Yes. She didn't believe her grandfather took those recipes from your grandfather and wanted the truth. It's my understanding that she talked to me, Donald Schuster, Paula Meyers and Theodore Henry."

Chase recognized all the names except one. "Theodore Henry?"

"Yes, he was the cook for Schuster at the time I worked for your grandfather." She sighed deeply before saying, "Theodore and I were lovers."

Chase's eyes widened and he leaned forward from his desk. "You were?"

"Yes," she admitted. "We were together for almost a year, but we kept things a secret. He felt his job as a cook with Mr. Schuster was on shaky ground and was desperate. He asked me to find a way to take those recipes. At first I wouldn't do it. I liked Mr. Graham for getting me the job and I thought your grandfather was a nice man, although he could be rather bullheaded at times."

Chase nodded. He knew his grandfather could definitely be that. "But you eventually took them, Ms. Evans?"

She nervously clutched the straps on her purse as tears filled her eyes. "Yes. I'm the one who gave them to Theodore. I got upset that Mr. Westmoreland let Mr. Graham go and wanted to do something to lash out at him. One day he left his recipe book out on his desk while he was out making deliveries. I made copies and passed them on to Theodore."

Chase was surprised; usually his grandfather had kept the family recipe book under lock and key. The old man must have had a lot on his mind that particular day. "I appreciate you coming and telling me the truth. It's finally put a lot of ill feelings to rest."

"Then it's not too late?" she asked, wiping her tears.

He reached across his desk to hand her a tissue. "Too late for what?"

"You and Ms. Claiborne. She told me that she loved you and wanted to tell you the truth, but had wanted to prove her grandfather's innocence first so that you would believe her."

Chase leaned back in his chair, feeling lower than low. Jessica had tried to tell him the truth but he hadn't listened. A bad feeling erupted in the pit of his stomach. What if she wouldn't forgive him for not believing her? What if she didn't want any part of him?

"Mr. Westmoreland?"

Chase took a deep breath and realized he hadn't answered the woman's question. "No, it's not too late. I love Jessica and together we can work out anything."

He had said the words, and he hoped to God that they were true.

* * *

Jessica noticed Chase's sports car the moment she pulled into the parking lot. Her stomach fluttered nervously as she gathered her purse and shopping bag to go inside her shop.

Moments later, barely after she'd gotten inside and closed the door behind her, there was a knock. She opened the door to find an older gentleman standing there. "Flowers for Jessica Claiborne."

Jessica smiled. It would be just like Jennifer to send her flowers to cheer her up, she thought, gazing lovingly at the huge vase of beautiful red roses. There seemed to be two dozen of them. "Thanks," she said. "If you wait a moment I'll get you a tip."

The old man grinned. "No need. It's been taken care of." His grin then widened. "He's never sent a woman flowers before. At least not from our shop."

Jessica lifted a puzzled arched eyebrow. "Who?"

The man chuckled. "I can't say, but he signed the card, and since he's aware of my wife's penchant to gab, I'm sure he knows that word of this delivery will be all over Atlanta before the sun goes down today. But evidently he doesn't care about that. Good day, ma'am." And then the man walked off and Jessica watched him get into a van from Coleman's Florist.

Closing the door behind her, a puzzled Jessica walked over to the counter, put the flowers down and pulled out the card.

Love makes you do and say foolish things.
I'm sorry,
Chase

Jessica didn't move. She barely breathed. Chase had sent the flowers to apologize! Before she could gather her thoughts there was another knock on her door. She quickly crossed the room to open it and found Donna standing there smiling.

"Hello, Jessica. I have a delivery for you, compliments of Chase's Place," she said, handing Jessica a huge bag. The aroma let Jessica know that whatever was inside would be delicious.

Jessica smiled, accepting the bag. "There's enough food here to feed two people."

Donna chuckled. "I think that's the idea."

Before Jessica could say anything, Donna was gone. Closing the door behind her, Jessica walked over to the counter and placed the bag of food next to the flowers. Before she could take a look inside, there was another knock at the door. For a moment she didn't move. Her heart knew. Her body knew. Her soul knew.

It was Chase.

Taking a deep breath she forced her body to cross the room. She exhaled deeply before gripping the handle to slowly open the door.

He stood there, leaning in the doorway holding a bottle of wine in his hand. He looked sexy, good enough to eat. Out of habit she licked her lips and watched his gaze move to her mouth. Her stomach clenched and her pulse spiked.

He didn't appear angry. That was a good thing. She inhaled deeply, knowing she needed either to ask him in or to ask him to leave. "Would you like to come in?"

"Yes." He hadn't hesitated in responding.

She swallowed hard and stepped aside to let him in. Where was extra oxygen when you needed it? she wondered, closing the door behind him. She leaned against the closed door knowing if she took one step she would fall. Her knees were too weak to support her. At this moment, she thought Chase looked more devastatingly handsome than he'd ever been before.

"Thanks for the flowers," she decided to say. "And for the food."

"You're welcome, and this is for you, too," he said, handing the bottle of wine to her.

She took his offering. "Thanks." It was only then that she forced herself away from the door to walk across the room to place the bottle of wine next to the flowers and delicious food. She slowly turned around and he was there, next to her. She hadn't heard him move. The look in his eyes was filled with regret.

"I'm sorry. I should have listened to you. I should have believed you," he whispered brokenly.

"I'm sorry, too," she said as a lump filled her throat. "I should have told you the truth as soon as I knew who you were."

He took another step to close the distance separating them. "I had three days to think about things. To think about us. And I want there to be an us, Jessica. What happened between our grandfathers is in the past. And you were right. Carlton didn't take the Westmoreland recipes. Darcy Evans came to see me earlier today. She came here first and found the shop closed. She wanted you to know the truth. She was the one who took the recipes. She and

Theodore Henry were lovers and she took them to get back at my grandfather for letting your grandfather quit."

Jessica tensed and took a step back. She met his gaze. "Is that why you're here? Because Darcy's words proved my innocence?"

Chase shook his head. "No. Even before Darcy came to see me I had made up my mind about us. I knew that I loved you. You don't have a deceitful or unethical bone in your body. You're nothing like Iris and I'm sorry I ever thought it. Please forgive me."

She met his gaze. They had both made mistakes. "I'll only forgive you if you forgive me for not being completely honest with you from the beginning. But I was so determined to prove my grandfather's innocence. I promised my grandmother on her deathbed that I would."

"And you did."

Jessica was filled with emotion at the thought that she truly had. She inhaled deeply as Chase covered the distance between them and reached out and lifted her chin with his finger.

"I love you, Jessica. I love you so much." He gathered her into his arms and whispered, "And I want forever with you. I want to put an end to the bitterness between our families. I want to form a new Westmoreland and Graham partnership. Please marry me. I want to give you my babies, love you, protect you, till death do us part and even after that."

"Oh, Chase," she said as tears burned her eyes. "I want all those things, too."

The smile Chase gave her would endear him to her forever. And then she felt herself being lifted into big strong arms. "We'll eat later," he whispered against her lips as he carried her up the stairs.

She shivered with need as he placed her on the bed. Then he was on the bed with her, kissing her, removing her clothes. She was filled with desire and love; her pulse skittered with need so overbearing it took her breath away.

When she was completely naked he stood to remove his own clothes. But she wanted to do more than watch. She wanted to help. She eased out of bed and helped him take off his sweater. Next was his belt. Then she unzipped his pants so he could strip out of them. When he stood before her wearing nothing but a sexy pair of briefs, she reached out and skimmed her hand down his chest, moving lower to his stomach, needing to touch him to make sure she wasn't dreaming.

And then she eased down on her knees to remove the last piece of clothing that shielded his body. She took her time, easing the briefs down his legs. Then she placed a kiss on his navel before leaning back and meeting his gaze.

"Come here," he whispered hoarsely, holding his hand out to her.

He gently tugged her to her feet, held her close in his arms and she felt his engorged arousal press into her quivering stomach.

She met his gaze. "I wanted to—"

"I know," he said, cutting off her words and pulling her closer. "But had I allowed you to do that, things would have been over before they'd gotten started. You're still new at all of this, and I'm going to enjoy spending the rest of my life exploring things with you."

He grinned down at her. "There will never be a dull moment at our house. You are and forever will be my most delicious craving."

Jessica's entire body swelled with love. "Make love to me, Chase," she whispered hotly against his lips.

He swept her back into his arms and placed her on the bed and joined her there. She shivered as need, strong and potent, raced through her. He pulled her into his arms, promising her a voyage into ecstasy and she knew that he was right—there would never be a dull moment at their house. And that they would spend the rest of their lives together.

She might be his delicious craving, but he was definitely her most ardent chocolate delight.

Epilogue

Two months later,
Christmas Day

Jessica smiled at her sister who was asking questions a mile a minute. It was her wedding day and she couldn't wait to join her life with Chase's. They had decided that since all the Westmorelands came home for the holidays, today would be perfect. And it was.

"Slow down, Savannah, and let me answer your first question," she chuckled. "His name is Durango Westmoreland and he's Chase's cousin. He works as a park ranger in Montana."

She watched the interest in her sister's eyes. It had been there since the rehearsal dinner last night when Durango, whose plane had been late, had arrived at Chase's Place, proving without a doubt that all the Westmoreland men were sexy.

"Now are you going to help me put on my veil or are you going to continue to stand there in a daze?" Jessica asked her sister.

Savannah laughed as she stepped behind Jessica and tugged the veil in place. "You look beautiful, Jess."

Jessica smiled. She actually felt beautiful. She glanced at Savannah's reflection in the mirror. Her sister was beautiful too, with hazel eyes, skin the color of caramel and long, wavy black hair that flowed down her back.

Jessica had also noticed Durango checking her sister out last night, but he'd kept his distance.

"Durango doesn't like city women," she said, turning around to face her sister.

Savannah lifted a brow. "Why?"

Jessica shrugged. "Something to do with an old wound. And sister of mine, you're definitely city."

It was Savannah's turn to shrug. She then smiled. "I guess he'll have to learn to like us. Because after seeing him, I've decided I definitely have a thing for mountain men."

Jessica raised her eyes to the ceiling. She didn't know who would need her prayers more: Durango or Savannah. Deciding she didn't want to dwell on that, she smiled, knowing she only had a few moments left before she became Chase's wife.

She and Chase had wanted a small ceremony, but it seemed the Westmorelands didn't know the meaning of small—three hundred plus guests had been invited. With everyone's help they had pulled things off in two months. Savannah was her maid of honor and Chase's cousin Quade was his best man.

The two sisters hugged. "I'm happy for you, Jess," Savannah whispered brokenly.

"Thanks. Chase is a good man. I'm getting the best." She pulled back and gazed lovingly at her sister. "One day it will be your time."

Savannah chuckled and a mischievous glint appeared in her eyes. "Let's not hold our breath for that to happen."

Oh, God, she's beautiful, Chase thought as he watched Jessica walk down the aisle toward him on her brother's arm. He was filled with emotion and had to fight back the lump in his throat and the mistiness in his eyes.

When she reached his side he saw her tears of joy, lifted her hands to his lips and whispered, "I love you."

He saw her smile through her tears. She was making him the happiest man on earth today by becoming his wife. Together, they turned to face the minister. Before he started speaking, Chase spoke up and said, "I do."

The minister lifted a brow. "You do?"

Chase nodded. "Yes."

The minister, who had known Chase since birth smiled. "I haven't asked any questions yet, Chase."

"Doesn't matter. 'I do' to all of them." At his side, he heard a snort and knew it had come from Quade.

The minister's smile widened. "Nevertheless, we will go through the ceremony as planned."

A short while later the minister said, "I now pronounce you man and wife. You may kiss your bride, Chase."

And he did. He turned and gathered Jessica into his arms. There was nothing gentle about the kiss. He totally ignored the fact that he was standing before three hundred guests as he devoured his wife's mouth.

Durango…or maybe it was Storm…tugged on his tux tails and said, "Leave something for later, will you?"

Chase let go of Jessica's mouth and looked at her, then returned her smile and whispered, "I couldn't help it, sweetheart. You're simply delicious."

* * * * *

Trust Me

by **Caroline Cross**

Imprisoned on a tropical
island by a ruthless dictator, aid
worker Lilah Cantrell finds that her
only hope for rescue is retrieval
specialist Dominic Steele--the man
who broke her heart years ago.
But can she trust him to keep
her safe...from him?

On sale
December 2005

Only from Silhouette Books.

If you enjoyed what you just read,
then we've got an offer you can't resist!

Take 2 bestselling
love stories FREE!
Plus get a FREE surprise gift!

Clip this page and mail it to Silhouette Reader Service™

IN U.S.A.	IN CANADA
3010 Walden Ave.	P.O. Box 609
P.O. Box 1867	Fort Erie, Ontario
Buffalo, N.Y. 14240-1867	L2A 5X3

YES! Please send me 2 free Silhouette Desire® novels and my free surprise gift. After receiving them, if I don't wish to receive anymore, I can return the shipping statement marked cancel. If I don't cancel, I will receive 6 brand-new novels every month, before they're available in stores! In the U.S.A., bill me at the bargain price of $3.80 plus 25¢ shipping and handling per book and applicable sales tax, if any*. In Canada, bill me at the bargain price of $4.47 plus 25¢ shipping and handling per book and applicable taxes**. That's the complete price and a savings of at least 10% off the cover prices—what a great deal! I understand that accepting the 2 free books and gift places me under no obligation ever to buy any books. I can always return a shipment and cancel at any time. Even if I never buy another book from Silhouette, the 2 free books and gift are mine to keep forever.

225 SDN DZ9F
326 SDN DZ9G

Name		(PLEASE PRINT)	
Address		Apt.#	
City	State/Prov.		Zip/Postal Code

Not valid to current Silhouette Desire® subscribers.

Want to try two free books from another series?
Call 1-800-873-8635 or visit www.morefreebooks.com.

* Terms and prices subject to change without notice. Sales tax applicable in N.Y.
** Canadian residents will be charged applicable provincial taxes and GST.
  All orders subject to approval. Offer limited to one per household.
  ® are registered trademarks owned and used by the trademark owner and or its licensee.

DES04R   ©2004 Harlequin Enterprises Limited

A new drama unfolds for
six of the state's wealthiest bachelors.

THE SECRET DIARY

This newest installment concludes with

A MOST SHOCKING REVELATION

by Kristi Gold

(Silhouette Desire, #1695)

Valerie Raines is determined to keep her mission
secret from Sheriff Gavin O'Neal. And that's easier
said than done when she's living in his house.
Especially when he's determined to seduce her!

*Available December 2005
at your favorite retail outlet.*

Silhouette Desire

COMING NEXT MONTH

#1693 NAME YOUR PRICE—Barbara McCauley
Dynasties: The Ashtons
His family's money and power tore them apart, but will time be able to heal the wounds of this priceless love?

#1694 TRUST ME—Caroline Cross
Men of Steele
An ex-navy SEAL is in over his head when he has to rescue the woman who broke his heart years ago.

#1695 A MOST SHOCKING REVELATION—Kristi Gold
Texas Cattleman's Club: The Secret Diary
A sexy sheriff is torn between his duty and his desire for a woman looking for her own brand of justice.

#1696 A BRIDE BY CHRISTMAS—Joan Elliott Pickart
Is this wedding planner really cursed never to find true love—or has Mr. Right just not appeared…until now?

#1697 TYCOON TAKES REVENGE—Anna DePalo
An infamous playboy gives a gossip columnist a taste of her own medicine, but finds that love is far sweeter than revenge.

#1698 TROPHY WIVES—Jan Colley
What will this wounded millionaire find beneath this rich girl's carefree facade?

SDCNM1105